THINKING OF YOU

"I had a wonderful time, Paul. Thanks." Fran's eyes glistened in the dark. Then, just as Paul was about to put his arms around her, the porch lights flashed on.

Fran stiffened. "Aunt Jane, this is Paul—"

"I know who he is," she cut Fran off abruptly. "What I want to know is where Ajit is. You had a date with him tonight."

Fran just wanted to die. She couldn't believe that the most wonderful day of her entire life was going to end like this. But before her aunt could say anything else, the sound of approaching footsteps caught her attention. Her sister and Ajit were walking up the path hand in hand.

Thinking Of You

Jeanette Nobile

BANTAM BOOKS
TORONTO • NEW YORK • LONDON • SYDNEY

RL 6, IL age 11 and up

THINKING OF YOU
A Bantam Book / July 1982

Cover photo by Pat Hill.

*Sweet Dreams and its associated logo are
trademarks of Bantam Books, Inc.*

ISBN 0-553-22516-2

Published simultaneously in the United States and Canada

*Bantam Books are published by Bantam Books, Inc. Its trademark,
consisting of the words "Bantam Books" and the portrayal of a rooster,
is Registered in U.S. Patent and Trademark Office and in other countries.
Marca Registrada. Bantam Books, Inc., 666 Fifth Avenue, New York,
New York 10103.*

PRINTED IN THE UNITED STATES OF AMERICA

0 9 8 7 6 5 4 3 2 1

*For Dith
and
Hunter girls
everywhere*

Chapter 1

Fran Pastore looked up at her aunt standing in front of the class, then bent her head down and let her long, bushy, chestnut hair fall forward. Fran often let her hair fall like this, creating her own little shelter against trouble. She did it now because she knew what was coming.

"Flynn!" Ms. Jane Harrigan called out as she began handing back the corrected American history final exams.

Doug Flynn saw his grade written boldly in red at the top of his exam and sighed, running a hand through his sandy blond hair in frustration.

"Davis!" Ms. Harrigan pronounced, flipping the next exam to Rena Davis, who glanced at it nonchalantly.

"Williamson!" Jane Harrigan didn't look up once as she returned the exams, refusing to display either pleasure or displeasure with the test results. It was typical of her. Over the years she had become known as the American History Teaching Machine. Her straight, light blond hair never dared to fall out of place after it was properly tied back. Her huge tortoise-shell glasses always sat up diligently on her sharp nose, serving those tiny but keen, all-seeing eyes. Jane Harrigan's mouth was a short, horizontal line that hardly ever curved into a smile. Standing at least five-foot-eight without heels, she used her height to search out cheaters, talkers, and gum chewers. Needless to say, Ms. Harrigan was not the most popular teacher at Medford High. And being her niece certainly hadn't helped Fran's social life this year. It was bad enough having everyone refer to her as "the smartest kid in school," but being related to Ms. Harrigan made it worse. Fran was sure the boys in her class thought Ms. Harrigan would shave points off their history grades if they even looked at Fran the wrong way, let alone asked her out.

"Danzig!" the voice went on.

Fran was filled with dread—she knew it was coming. She shot a quick, nervous look back at Paul Wingate, her latest crush. But of course he didn't even notice her. Her large, dark brown eyes glistened with anxiety, and she bit her lip tensely.

2

"Pastore!" the voice announced.

Fran wanted to jump out the window and escape. But there was nothing she could do now.

Ms. Harrigan walked over to Fran's desk and handed her her exam.

"Good work, Frances. A plus." Ms. Harrigan peered down at Fran over her glasses and smiled.

"Thank you," Fran mumbled, staring at her exam. She couldn't have been more embarrassed.

No wonder everyone hates me! Fran thought to herself in a fury. *It's because of her, because of the way she treats me. I don't want to be a genius. Why does she have to announce my grades like that? She doesn't do it to anyone else. She makes me feel like a freak. I wish I were stupid. Maybe she'd leave me alone, then. What must Paul think of me? I hate this!*

Ms. Harrigan continued to pass out the exams. No other students were complimented for good grades, even though Fran refused to believe that she was the only one in class to get an A. Fran just stared down at her desk top. She wished a giant bird would fly through the window, pick her up from her desk, and take her away to China. Any place that was away from her aunt.

It was the last period on the last day of school, and the students were understandably more eager to be dismissed than usual. But Ms.

Harrigan wasn't finished yet. No one really expected her to let class out early, though, because Ms. Harrigan wasn't like the other teachers. She was the Teaching Machine. There were five minutes left in the period, and she intended to use them.

"Now," she stated, calling the class to attention, "you have officially completed American History I. Well, at least some of you have," she said, as she glanced at Doug Flynn. "As seniors next September, you will be enrolled in American History II—something you will all look forward to, I'm sure. American History II will pick up right where we left off with this class—Reconstruction—and will take you through World War II and, time permitting, cover the Korean and Vietnam wars."

Fran could hear a lot of annoyed sighs around her. *Only Aunt Jane would lecture on the last day of school. A great send-off for the junior class. What did I ever do to deserve her?*

"Since I will be teaching American History II next year—"

A collective groan of agony rose from the class at the thought of another year with Ms. Harrigan.

Jane Harrigan chose to ignore their reaction, however, and went right on with her lecture. "—I've decided that it would be wise not to waste any time and start right in with a brief

4

preview of the course. Now, as you know, America was still mending its wounds after the Civil War, and President Grant . . ."

Undaunted by the glares and moans from her class, Ms. Harrigan continued to talk until the bell rang. Everyone stampeded to the door—everyone except Fran, who didn't want to hear what her classmates were saying about her aunt. But as she gathered up her books, she noticed that Paul Wingate and Doug Flynn had stayed behind, too. Paul went over to Doug, who looked very depressed. Fran couldn't hear what they were saying, but it was obvious from Paul's concerned expression and his hand on Doug's shoulder that he was consoling Doug for having flunked history. Fran felt guilty by association.

What a nice guy Paul was, she thought to herself. Not only was he tall and good-looking, but he really seemed to care about people. If only she had a chance with a boy like that.

Then, out of the corner of her eye, Fran spotted her aunt at her desk. Naturally, she was in no mood to talk to her right now. In fact, she didn't even want to be seen with her in public. Going straight to the girl's locker room, Fran quietly began to empty out her locker, sticking worn paperbacks, old sweat socks, various spray cans and plastic bottles, and Harry, her stuffed koala bear, into a big canvas tote bag.

"Hey, Fran!"

Fran jumped, startled by the unexpected voice, then turned.

"It's me, Fran. Your own flesh and blood. Oh, how quickly they forget!"

It was Maggie, Fran's younger sister. Five-foot-two, with a button nose, short black curls, and sapphire eyes, Maggie was a natural flirt. Dressed in her skintight Calvins and lacy pink camisole, she was irresistible. Add to that her outrageous sense of humor and the boys of Medford High didn't have a chance. Unfortunately, Fran wasn't in the mood for Maggie at that moment. "Hi, Maggie," she mumbled.

"Hey, what's wrong, Fran?"

"Nothing."

"Come on, Fran. I know something's bugging you. You can't fool me." Although nobody thought of Maggie as smart, she often seemed much wiser than her older sister. A year younger than Fran, Maggie often gave Fran advice. "You want to tell me about it, Fran?" she asked gently.

"Guess," Fran mumbled.

"Don't tell me. Aunt Jane?" It wasn't hard for Maggie to guess, since there was only one person who could get the usually mild-mannered Fran this upset.

"Who else?" Fran said.

"What's she done now?"

"Her usual—humiliate me in front of everybody. Now they hate me more than ever."

"Nobody *hates* you, Fran."

"Wrong. Everybody hates me because they think I'm a brain and because Aunt Jane treats me like I'm better than everyone else. That's why no one likes me."

"Oh, come on, Fran. Aren't you exaggerating just a little bit?"

"Exaggerating!? Do you remember what she did to David Cooper? The first boy who ever liked me! He walked me home from school, and we were just beginning to really talk—he would have asked me out if Aunt Jane hadn't embarrassed me right in front of him. She started telling him about how smart I was and how much studying I did and how I didn't have time for all the usual teenage foolishness because 'gifted' students can't waste their talents. I'm sick of being called gifted. David almost ran out the door after that, and he's been afraid to look at me ever since. And who could blame him? Would you want to go out with the Abominable Brain?"

Maggie tried not to smile at Fran's remark. "Oh, Fran, I don't know what to say anymore. I know she's awful, only she doesn't think so. She thinks she's protecting you."

"I know she *thinks* she's helping me, but she isn't. She's making my life miserable."

"Yeah, I know. And anytime we try to tell her to lighten up on you, she just says that looking out for us is her responsibility. I wonder if she was this bad before Mom died."

"Who knows? I just wish she'd stop talking about it. I mean, I know they were the only two sisters in the family, just like us, but Mom wouldn't have wanted it this way. She's nothing like Mom. Mom wouldn't—" Then all of a sudden Fran stopped talking as a tear trickled down her cheek. The only thing she could focus on was her memory of that grainy newspaper photograph of her mother's demolished station wagon and the horrible headlines proclaiming her death.

Maggie put her arm around Fran's shoulders and gently brushed the thick hair away from her face. "Come on, Fran. Stop crying. That was a long time ago, and we both know that things would have been a lot different if the accident had never happened. But we can't change that now. I mean, Aunt Jane is a pain and all, but you know Dad's on our side. Whenever she really gets out of control, Dad puts her in her place."

"For you, he does. But it's different with me."

"What do you mean?" Maggie asked defensively.

"I'm the 'genius'—the one with the high IQ! You can talk to Dad. But with me, he's—I don't know—more careful. He always has to consult with Aunt Jane when it comes to me. She's got

8

him convinced that I'm some kind of fragile computer that'll be damaged if he interferes too much."

"That's not true," Maggie snapped back. "The only reason Dad doesn't help you more is because *you* never tell him what's bothering you. With you, everything's a big secret. You always keep everything bottled up inside. I swear, if I didn't pry you open every once in a while, you'd explode."

Maggie looked at Fran sternly, but Fran just stared into the shadows of her locker. She knew Maggie was right. She was always afraid to rock the boat, afraid to confront her aunt and challenge her, afraid to reveal her true feelings. Fran envied her sister for her ability to speak up when things bothered her. Aunt Jane never bossed Maggie around, and Maggie and their father could talk easily, more like pals than father and daughter.

Suddenly Fran didn't want to think anymore. She threw her arms around her sister and hugged her tightly. Maggie was the only one who really understood her and cared.

"All right, all right. Let's not make a soap opera out of this," Maggie said, laughing. "Come on, Fran. Wipe your eyes and finish up what you were doing here so we can go home. Okay? Hey, it's summer. Smile!"

Fran lifted her head and pushed the unruly

strands of hair out of her puffy red eyes. She smiled weakly and sniffed.

Turning back to her locker, she threw a few last books into her tote, then looked at the pictures taped to the inside of her locker door. One was of Al Pacino and the other of a young Laurence Olivier in the role of Heathcliff from the old movie version of *Wuthering Heights* that she loved so much. Impulsively she reached up and ripped them both down, then crumpled them up into a ball.

"What did you do that for?" Maggie asked, surprised.

"I've just decided. I'm going to be a nun." She picked up her bulging tote and walked to the trash can to deposit Laurence and Al. "Come on, let's go home."

Maggie just stood where she was, regarding her sister with disbelief. From the back, Fran was a strange sight—shapeless brown cords frayed at the heels, a plain beige blouse that fit like a supermarket shopping bag, and that indescribable mop of hair. Maggie just shook her head as she thought of the wonderful figure and those gorgeous big eyes that Fran kept hidden. "What am I going to do with you, Fran?" she whispered under her breath, rolling her eyes to the ceiling.

Fran pushed through the front door of the Pastore home—a big, three-story house full of real, dark-stained wood paneling and handcarved trim. Everyone said that walking into the Pastore's front parlor was almost like walking into the past. Almost. Today it was Maggie's lavender roller skates with the bright yellow wheels sitting at the foot of the heavy mahogany banister in the hallway and her pile of *Seventeen* magazines strewn over the Oriental rug in the parlor that betrayed the fact that this was really Medford, Massachusetts, in the 1980s and not Beacon Hill at the turn of the century.

Maggie rushed in right behind Fran, sticking to her like glue, demanding an answer to the question she had just asked. "But why not, Fran? Just tell me why not."

"Because. That's all." Fran wouldn't look at her sister. She wished Maggie would just go away and leave her alone for a while.

"I don't understand you. First you tell me that boys run away from you. Then I offer you a great solution to your problem, and you won't even consider it. Why? Would it kill you to go to a hairdresser just to get a trim? Nothing dramatic. Just a little alteration so people could see your face."

"No." Fran was adamant.

"Why?"

"Because I hate beauty parlors—they smell like funeral parlors. Anyway, there's nothing wrong with my hair. If I have to look glamorous to get a boyfriend, I might as well give up because I'm just not the type."

"Fran, what's wrong with trying to look your best? Look, you've just got too much hair. No one can even see your face."

Fran turned her back on Maggie and went into the kitchen.

"Come on, Fran. Don't run away from me. I'm only trying to help you." Maggie followed closely behind Fran.

"Maggie, you know how I feel about clothes and makeup and all that. It all makes me very uncomfortable. If I go to your hairdresser, I'll just feel like I'm trying to be something I'm not."

"But the point is you're *not* being what you could be. You've got a beautiful face and a nice bod, but you insist on hiding yourself."

Fran blushed at Maggie's blunt assessment.

"Don't be ridiculous, Maggie. You're the beauty in this family, not me. Besides, my real problem is Aunt Jane. She's the one who keeps me a social outcast."

"You can't blame it all on Aunt Jane. Anyway, school is out. This is your chance to find out if you can have a normal relationship with someone."

"Yeah. That's what I said on the way home," Fran admitted defensively, "I do intend to stop acting like a nerd. What's wrong with that?"

"Nothing! I think it's great. The only problem is that you *look* like a nerd. Take a good look at yourself. You'll never get a boyfriend the way you dress."

"You're too kind." Fran gritted her teeth, dropping her heavy tote on the kitchen floor. "Do you want a yogurt?" she asked, turning to the refrigerator.

"Don't change the subject! I'm trying to help you, but you're too stupid to realize that. And they say I'm the dumb sister. Jeez!"

"Wait a minute, Maggie. Look at this."

A hastily scribbled note was taped to the refrigerator door. Maggie read over Fran's shoulder.

Girls,

Please set another place for dinner. Aunt Jane is coming over to discuss something "important" (she wouldn't tell me over the phone). I'll have some news for you, too. See you around 6:30.

Love,
Dad

"Oh, sh—"

"Don't say it," Fran interrupted. "I feel the same way."

Fran found two cups of yogurt in the refrigerator. "Lemon or blueberry?" she asked.

"Doesn't matter." Maggie sighed, disgusted with the prospect of dinner with her aunt, an event that was always more like a board meeting than a meal.

Glumly, the two girls sat down at the kitchen table and ate their yogurts in depressing silence. Most guests brought dessert to dinner; Aunt Jane always brought trouble.

Chapter 2

Maggie sat at the kitchen table, shelling peas, a large pile of empty pods on her left, a larger pile of unshelled pods on her right. The stainless steel bowl in front of her was only one-third full, but Maggie remained intent on her task.

In the meantime, Fran basted the chicken in the oven, then measured enough water for four servings of rice.

"Maggie," Fran asked as she put the pot of water on a back burner and turned on the flame, "should I make the rice with sauteed onions and mushrooms again?"

"Yeah, why not? Much better than plain old rice with butter." Maggie didn't look up from her shelling.

Fran stared at her for a second, wiping the

beads of sweat from her forehead. "Can I ask you something, Maggie?"

"Sure. What's that?"

"There was a head of broccoli in the refrigerator. Why did you run out to get peas? It's taking you forever to shell them."

"That's okay." Maggie was unfazed by Fran's comment.

"I don't get it. As I remember, you hate to cook anything that takes more than ten minutes to prepare."

"That's right." Maggie kept up her shelling pace as she talked.

"Then why are you fussing with all these silly peas?"

"Don't be stupid, Fran. Think!"

Fran frowned, unable to come up with a reason for her sister's sudden passion for peas.

Maggie looked up at Fran and grimaced in annoyance at her sister's poor memory. "Why would I go to all this trouble for peas, Fran? Who *hates* peas, Fran?"

"Oh, yeah! Aunt Jane hates peas!"

"Right! Now would you like to help?"

"Gladly." Fran took a seat and grabbed a handful of pea pods. "What do you think Aunt Jane is coming to discuss?"

"Who knows? But you know how she is. Remember the last time she came to dinner with something 'important' to discuss?"

"Yeah, I remember. Dad should have told

16

her off then. She's really got to be a little crazy to tell Dad that he has to make sure I only read hardcover books because the print in paperbacks is too small and it'll ruin my eyes. I can't imagine how she thinks up these things."

"Who knows? If she only knew about that pile of steamy paperbacks under your bed . . ."

"Quiet. That's just between you and me and the bed."

Just then the girls heard the front door open.

"Anybody home? Fran? Maggie?" It was Mr. Pastore, home from work.

"Hi, Dad. We're in the kitchen," Maggie yelled.

Jack Pastore walked into the kitchen, mimicking a weary businessman. "Hello, dears." He gave a mock sigh, "What's for dinner?"

"Aunt Jane," Fran said.

"Yuk! Let's go out for a pizza. How about it, Fran?"

Jack Pastore was always good-natured, always ready with a laugh or a funny remark. His large brown eyes would light up whenever he saw his daughters or met someone new, and the world's most contagious smile would take over his face. It was no wonder he had won the Pulitzer Prize for investigative reporting, Fran had always said. She imagined her father meeting a terrorist, taking him out for a beer, and within an hour, charming the most crucial secrets out of the guy. Maggie, on the other hand, always pictured him as the bumbling detective constantly searching through the pockets of his wrinkled raincoat for a pen and running his hand through his curly salt-and-pepper hair in confusion. People would underestimate him until he got back to his desk at the *Boston Globe*, where he'd write up his scathing exposés and shocking features, Maggie thought.

He stepped between his girls now and planted a big kiss on each head. But while Maggie received his kiss willingly, Fran pulled back a bit, embarrassed by her father's physical show of affection. "So besides the fact that the chairman of the board is coming to dinner, what else is new and exciting?" Mr. Pastore smiled. "Trying to corner the pea pod market?" He nodded toward the mounting pile of empty pods.

Fran shot a guilty look at her sister, but Maggie's expression remained innocent. "Peas are in season, Dad. I thought you liked peas?"

"Oh, I do, I do." If he was aware of the peas-for-Aunt-Jane caper, he wasn't letting on.

"So are you going to keep us in suspense until dinner?" Fran asked. "Or can we hear your news now?"

"You sure can," he enthused. "Your old man is going international. The *Globe* is sending me on assignment to Northern Ireland."

"You're kidding!" Maggie squealed.

"Sounds exciting—but dangerous," Fran added.

"Don't worry, Fran. I'm not covering the fighting. I'll be doing a feature series on two neighboring families in Belfast, the McGoons and the O'Days. The McGoons are Catholic, and the O'Days are Protestant, but they've remained friends despite the fighting. And their alliance goes back for centuries. They're something of a legend in Belfast. I'm going to live with them for a while, watch them at home, go to work with them, the whole number. I think it'll be a wonderful story for the *Globe.* People are killing each other all over the world, and yet these supposedly natural enemies support and respect each other to the hilt. I can't wait to meet them."

"Wow! It does sound like a great story," Fran agreed enthusiastically.

Maggie picked up the stainless steel bowl of peas and passed her hand over it as if it were a crystal ball. "I see a reporter—it is Jack Pastore! I see a newspaper—the *Boston Globe*! I see a five-part series on two Irish families. Wait! What is this? I see—a prize! The Pulitzer Prize—another Pulitzer for Jack Pastore!"

"Well, let's not jump the gun, Maggie," her father said, laughing. "It would be very nice, but I'm satisfied with the one Pulitzer I have."

"Are you kidding?" Maggie demanded. "Boston's number-one reporter? They should give you a six-pack of Pulitzers!"

"And they oughta give you an Oscar for this performance," he teased, then gave her a hug. "Now let's be serious for a minute. When do you start work at that record shop, Maggie?"

"Nine o'clock Monday morning, sir." Maggie gave him a salute and a wink.

"How about you, Fran? Any luck in the summer job search?"

"No." Fran sighed in despair. "I've tried everywhere, but no one seems to be hiring kids for the summer. Boy, Maggie, were you ever lucky to get a full-time summer job at Music Towne!"

"Not lucky. They had to give me a job," Maggie declared brazenly.

"What do you mean they *had* to give you a job?"

"It just stands to reason, Fran. I'm their best customer. I mean, I spent most of the money I made last summer in Music Towne. Hiring me is like an investment for them. Whatever money they pay me this summer, they're sure to get back by next spring."

"Very clever. Is that what you told them when you applied for the job?"

"Yup. Besides, they know how excited I get about new records. I'm like a dancing advertisement. People'll see me dancing to the new releases, and they'll have to buy them."

"Hmmmm." Mr. Pastore rubbed his chin. "I wonder if we could sell newspapers the same way. Plant people with big grins on their faces all over town and have them reading the *Globe*. Happy *Globe* readers in the flesh—I like it."

Maggie's eyes widened. "Yeah, and you could hire Fran to be the first happy *Globe* reader. You could go all around Boston, Fran, just smiling and holding a newspaper in front of you." Maggie grinned at the thought of her serious sister with a pasted-on smile like an airline stewardess's.

"Not funny," Fran said.

"But seriously, Fran," her father cut in, "what I was about to tell you was that the *Globe* has an apprenticeship program this summer. They're taking a dozen high-school students—six in July and six in August—to work in several departments of the paper. I hear the pay is pretty bad and the work is no more than go-fer duty—you know, getting things for people—but I think it would be interesting for you to see how a big daily operates. And it certainly wouldn't hurt to have that on a resumé or a college application. I brought the job application home just in case you were interested."

Fran's face lit up at the possibility of working at the *Globe.* It was the only good news she had had all day, but it made up for the rest. "Sure, I'm interested! I'll fill out the application tonight."

"Good. I hear they've already picked most of

the kids for July, but you've got a good shot at the August hiring."

"*Fan*-tastic!"

"Now, girls," Mr. Pastore said, his expression becoming serious, "I've got other news that may not thrill you."

"What is it?" A look of deep concern shaded Fran's face.

"While I'm away"—he hesitated—"Aunt Jane will be staying with you."

"Oh, no!" Maggie moaned.

"Why, Dad?" Fran protested. "Why can't Mrs. Sokol next door just look in on us? We don't need a babysitter."

"Well, it's not that I think you need a babysitter. I know you can take care of yourselves. It's just that I've never left you for more than two or three days at a time. I'll be gone at least a week, and if I run into problems in Belfast, I may have to stay there longer. I just don't like the thought of you two here alone for that long."

"Yeah, but why Aunt Jane?" Maggie protested. "I'd rather be left at the dog pound for the week."

"Oh, come on, Maggie. She's not that bad," Mr. Pastore objected.

"Wanna bet?" Fran muttered under her breath.

"Look, just stay out of her way, and things'll be fine. You'll be at work all day, Maggie. And,

Fran, I'm sure you can find something to do with yourself. Anyway, you know your aunt— she'll be out all the time. Between the symphony, the museums, and her antiquing, I doubt if you'll see that much of her."

"Will you put that in writing?" Maggie asked.

"All right, all right. I tell you what I'll do. After dinner tonight, the four of us will sit down and set the ground rules so there'll be no trouble. Okay? I'll make sure there will be peaceful coexistence, as the Russians used to say. You guys will mind your business, and Jane'll mind hers. That way there won't be any problems."

"Wanna bet?"

"Okay, Maggie, you're on. Five bucks says I straighten out this whole deal after dinner. If anything goes wrong when I'm away, you collect."

"You've got a bet, Dad." Maggie and her father shook on it.

But Fran just shook her head, a faraway look on her face. *Ten days with Aunt Jane— I'll never make it.* She glanced down at the bowl of peas and pursed her lips. "Come on, Maggie. Let's finish up these peas."

Maggie looked at all the peas and shot her a mischievous glance. Unfortunately, there wouldn't be much mischief or good times of any kind while Aunt Jane was around, Fran thought.

*   *   *

"That chicken was excellent, Fran," Mr. Pastore commented as Maggie cleared the dirty dishes from the table. "What do you call that recipe?"

"Coq au vin, Dad," Fran yelled from the kitchen.

Jane Harrigan frowned. "Do you mean to tell me, Jack, that you actually allow your children to cook with wine?"

He shrugged. "Sure. What's the matter? Don't you like French cuisine?"

"You know what I mean. I'm referring to the fact that they are both minors. It's wrong for them to drink. This could start them on the road to alcoholism. Don't you realize that?"

"Loosen up, will you, Jane? They aren't drinking it."

"Well, they won't have wine when I'm in charge," Jane declared.

"Let's not argue, Jane. The four of us have a lot to discuss, so let's not start out on the wrong foot, okay?"

"I only want what's best for the girls, Jack. You know that. My sister would have done the same."

Jack Pastore just sighed, refusing to credit that statement with a response. His wife had been as different from Jane as two people could be. In fact, when Mandi was alive, she had said she couldn't wait until the girls were old enough so she could teach them how to cook. Jane had little interest in fancy cooking, always saying that it was bad for one's health.

Mandi had been so fun-loving, while Jane was just the opposite. Mandi had passions for Red Sox games, rock 'n' roll, sad movies, and cookouts. Jane liked conservative Democrats, ballet, and unsalted butter. Mandi was always smiling; Jane rarely showed any emotion at all.

It was easy to see why maintaining peaceful relations with the self-appointed savior of his children had not been easy for Jack Pastore after his wife died. But when the girls entered high school and started spending every school day with Jane, it had become even more difficult for him. If Maggie wore a tiger-striped top to school or Fran was seen reading a romantic paperback, Jack was sure to get an angry call at the office from Jane. At one point, when Fran was a freshman, Jane had actually suggested that the girls move in with her, intimating that he was an unfit parent. But Jack was patient and understanding, telling himself that she wasn't being malicious. This was just her way of caring for her motherless nieces. Nevertheless, staring back at her steely gaze now, Jack began to have second thoughts about leaving Fran and Maggie at her mercy.

"Here we go!" Maggie sang out as she waltzed into the dining room with a small strawberry cheesecake on a serving platter.

"Hey, that looks good." Her father's eyes widened in anticipation.

"Bought it with my own two hands, Dad."

"I'm proud of you, daughter of mine." He chuckled.

Jane frowned down at the cake.

"What's wrong, Aunt Jane?" Maggie asked, holding back a grin. "Don't you like cheesecake? Aren't you feeling well? You didn't eat your peas, either."

"I'm quite well, thank you."

Just then Fran came in, balancing a tray of cups, dessert plates, and a pot of coffee.

"Okay, Jane, we're waiting for your news," Jack said, trying to be jovial. "You've got us on the edges of our seats."

Without a word, Jane took a cup and poured herself some black coffee. "None for me, thank you," she said to Maggie, who was now cutting the cheesecake. She picked up her cup and took a tiny sip of coffee, then set her cup down slowly and folded her hands on the table.

"Well, my news concerns Frances. I must say from the start that this was no mean accomplishment, but through a great deal of perseverance, I pulled it off."

"Get to the point, get to the point," Maggie muttered as she passed out slices of cake to her father and sister.

Jane ignored her younger niece and continued at her own deliberate pace. "Harvard is

26

sponsoring a special program this summer for gifted high-school juniors. It's an accelerated, intensive, comprehensive course that will enable the students to skip their senior years of high school and enter Harvard or Radcliffe a year early." Jane's normally short mouth stretched into a long, thin, Cheshire-cat grin. "And at the last minute, I've managed to get you into the program, Frances."

"What!?" Fran couldn't believe what she was hearing. How could her aunt have done something like this behind her back, without even asking her?

"You don't look very happy, Frances. I thought you'd be thrilled about such an exciting opportunity."

"Thank you," Fran murmured. She looked down into her coffee, and her hair fell forward, covering her face.

Maggie glared at her sister, wanting her to say what she felt. She was sure Fran didn't want to go to summer school and that she certainly didn't want to start college a year early. Maggie was furious with Fran's silence.

"You start the program on Monday morning, Frances," Jane announced triumphantly.

"Fran," her father asked softly, "do you want to go to this summer school?"

"Well—not really."

"Frances, think before you speak. This is

27

the chance of a lifetime. Finally you'll be able to exercise your full potential."

"I don't think she's interested in starting college in September, Jane."

"My reputation in the field of education is at stake here, Jack," she snapped. "Originally they didn't want to accept Frances into the program without a personal interview, and there wasn't time for that. I had to vouch for her high dedication and motivation to succeed. I'd look like a fool if Fran backed out now."

"What do you think, Fran?" her father asked.

"Well, I did sort of want to apply for the apprenticeship at the *Globe*, Dad."

"Frances, you *can't* say no," Jane said desperately. "Not only will you be hurting yourself, you will be humiliating me."

"But I—"

"How can you just toss the opportunity of a lifetime out the window?"

"Don't stack the deck against her, Jane," Jack stated firmly. "Since you really think this is important, I suggest that Fran try it out while I'm away on assignment. Frankly, I have a feeling that your time together will go a lot smoother if Fran doesn't refuse this program of yours out of hand. But when I get back from Belfast, we'll all discuss it again. If Fran doesn't like it, she can quit. Okay, Jane?"

"Of course she'll like it." Jane was confident.

"In the meantime, Fran," her father continued, "fill out the *Globe* apprenticeship application and send it in. You can always turn down the job if you do decide to stay with the summer school."

"Fill it out if you like, Frances, but I'm sure you'll change your mind about this program after you start."

"Don't worry about Fran, Jane. She'll make up her own mind. Now I'll expect everything to be nice and normal while I'm away. If nobody treads on anyone else's toes, it should be peaceful around here."

There was a tense silence in the room. Fran was jittery and anxious. Jack felt uneasy about leaving with this hostile attitude still lingering.

Only Maggie dared to break the silence. "More cheesecake, anyone?"

Chapter 3

The cab came to pick up their father around seven-thirty the next morning. Fran and Maggie walked him down to the curb, saying their good-byes and wishing him good luck.

"Now I want you two to have a good week, promise?" Mr. Pastore looked at his daughters, searching for signs of trouble.

"Don't worry, Dad. We'll be okay," Fran said, but not very convincingly.

"Yeah, we can keep Aunt Godzilla at bay while you're gone." Maggie nodded confidently.

"I'm going to pretend I didn't hear that, Maggie. When I'm in Belfast, I want to think that you're all getting along fine, playing Parcheesi by the crackling fire."

31

"Parcheesi with Aunt Jane?" Maggie laughed. "That'll be the day."

"Okay, I know she's a pain, but do your best. Don't pick fights with her, but don't let her push you around, either. That goes double for you, Fran. Remember, if you don't like summer school by the time I get back, you can quit."

"Okay, Dad." Fran forced a weak smile.

"I love you two, and I'm going to miss you." He hugged them tightly and kissed them. "Be good and take care. I'll see you a week from Monday." Mr. Pastore got into the cab and told the driver to take him to Logan Airport.

The girls stood at the curb and watched the cab drive down the street until it took a right turn and disappeared.

"Boy, you're really dumb," Maggie commented matter-of-factly.

"You told me that last night." Fran sighed.

"I know, but I feel obliged to tell you again."

"Why?"

"Because Dad gave you the opportunity to say no to Aunt Jane's summer-school scheme, but you didn't say anything. You sat there like a little martyr. And just now he was practically begging for you to say 'I don't want to go.' "

"He was not," Fran snapped icily.

"He was so." Maggie raised her voice.

"You make it sound so simple," Fran said

angrily. "Do you really think I could just say 'No, Aunt Jane, I don't want to go to your special summer program'? Do you think she'd leave it at that? No way, Maggie. She'd be hounding me around the clock if I refused to go."

"So you're just gonna go along with it? No matter how unhappy it makes you?"

"No! I'll go for a while. Then if I hate it, I'll quit."

"*Sure* you will!" Maggie said.

"Why do you doubt me all the time?" Fran was hurt by her sister's attitude.

"Fran, you know I'm always behind you, no matter what. But frankly you're a wimp. I mean, it's really your own fault that you're always so unhappy."

"What do you mean?" Fran asked defensively.

"You don't stand up for yourself because you're afraid of what other people will think of you. You don't want to confide in Dad, and you're afraid to talk back to Aunt Jane—"

"But you know how she is," Fran cut in. "She gets hysterical, makes a big scene if I don't do what she wants."

"So what? Let her make a big scene. She's the one who'll look stupid."

"That's not true. She embarrasses me in front of other kids, especially boys. You remember what she did to David Cooper—"

"Yeah, yeah, I know all about David Cooper. You tell me about that all the time. But are you going to give up on boys just because she embarrassed you once?"

"N-no . . ." Fran knew she was losing to Maggie's plain common sense. There was nothing that Maggie was saying that Fran hadn't argued to herself many times in the past. She desperately wanted to tell her aunt to leave her alone, but something always kept her from fighting back.

"Look, I don't mean to hurt you," Maggie said. "I just want to prove to you that things aren't always as hopeless as you think."

Fran sighed deeply. "You're probably right." Then they started walking back toward the house in silence.

"Hey," Maggie said as they reached the front steps, "what time is Aunt Jane coming over this morning?"

"She said she'd be here sometime after ten." Fran moaned.

"Then let's go out. Let's spend the day in Harvard Square. She's got her own key, so there's no reason for us to hang around here."

Fran considered the proposition for a moment. A day in the square was one day less spent with Aunt Jane, she figured.

"Why not?" Fran said with conviction. "Let's go!"

*   *   *

The bus let them off right in front of the Coop in the heart of Harvard Square. It was a typical Saturday morning in the square, with hundreds of people meandering through the shops, looking at the wares of the numerous street vendors, and spilling out into the streets despite the threatening traffic. The cars inched forward impatiently, constantly jostling for a better position only to be confronted with unexpected one-way streets or packs of pedestrians.

The moment they stepped off the bus Fran and Maggie became part of the scene, thrilled to be where so much was happening. Even their aunt was forgotten for the moment.

"Shall we take a look around the Coop?" Maggie suggested.

Fran nodded enthusiastically.

Although it was a department store originally started specifically for Harvard students and faculty, everyone shopped at the Coop. Fran liked the Coop because they had three floors of books in the Annex. Maggie liked it because they had pretty good clothes and a fantastic record department—though, in her opinion, not quite as good as Music Towne. The front of the Coop, the old building, had a large, marble-floored entranceway lined with windows that always displayed headless mannequins in tweed jackets, navy blazers, and seersucker suits. Street musicians and political activists usually occupied this vestibule, and today a young man with a long red beard was there playing classical guitar. His guitar case was open at his side, and occasionally people would toss coins into it. Maggie and Fran stopped to listen for a moment.

"This is pretty good," Maggie commented. "I could probably get into this classical stuff. What do you think he's playing? Beethoven?"

"Bach's Bourrée in E minor," Fran corrected.

Maggie frowned at her sister. "Know-it-all!"

"Sorry." Fran flushed. "I just happened to know that one."

"Sure, sure. Come on, let's go in."

Maggie pushed through the old glass door and through the crowded aisles to the women's department. By the time Fran caught up with her, Maggie had already found her way to a rack of camisoles. She whipped a satiny, peach-colored one off the circular rack and looked at it.

"What do you think?" she asked, not looking up at Fran.

"You've got one just like it, Maggie."

"Not for me, Einstein! For you." Maggie whisked the camisole around and held it up over Fran's shapeless Medford High T-shirt.

Fran immediately pushed it away. "Don't be ridiculous!" she said. There was real anger in her voice.

"Why? I think you'd look pretty in it."

"I would not. That's your style, Maggie, not mine!"

"You're so—hopeless!" Maggie sputtered. "Look at you. If you stopped dressing like a nerd, maybe guys would notice how pretty you are!"

"Stop it, Maggie! I know I've got to make some changes, but let me do it my way, okay?"

"Oh, you're just making excuses again. Come on, go try this on. I'll find you a pair of nice tight jeans to go with it."

Fran glared at her sister, her nostrils flaring. "Absolutely not." She turned and marched out the back door, heading for the Annex.

Watching Fran's stubborn figure maneuver around the racks of clothes and the glass counters, stray wisps of her hair flagging behind her, Maggie was instantly sorry that she had pushed her sister so far this time.

But she knew where Fran was headed—the second floor of the Coop Annex, where the paperbacks were. That was fine with Maggie because the big record department was on the same floor. While Fran lost herself among the romantic novels, Maggie would be content to rummage through the bins of rock albums.

Fran now mounted the escalator to the second floor, still furious with Maggie—and with herself for losing her temper. *Okay, maybe I*

*don't have to wear baggy T-shirts all the time,
but I'm really not the camisole type—so what
type am I?*

As the escalator glided up to the second
floor, Fran immediately forgot about Maggie and
her criticisms. Her eyes glowed with anticipation as she surveyed the long shelves of books.
If there was any place in the world where Fran
would be a happy prisoner, it was the second
floor of the Coop. Other girls had passions for
clothes and records; Fran had it for novels.

She had a well-established method of browsing here. First, she examined the New and Noteworthy section. Then, the display tables. Finally,
she combed through the general fiction section,
searching for her favorite authors and books
that just caught her eye.

The New and Noteworthy section was a disappointment today. Weird science fiction. Cat
books. Several rather unappetizing cookbooks
that proclaimed the wonders of either soy beans,
tofu, or celery. Quick and easy diet books.

Fran moved on to the display tables. Here
she found rock 'n' roll books, books on repair-
ing cars and bicycles, and an assortment of
oversized picture books.

Then she walked to the end of the long
fiction section along the wall and started to
scan the shelves. On a bottom shelf, there was
a book that caught Fran's eye. It was called *The*

Heart of the Wild by someone named Anton Browne. Fran had never heard of the book or its author before, but the cover was enough to intrigue her. It was a pen-and-ink sketch of a young man with large, soulful eyes and a set, determined mouth. A forest was sketched in the background, the dark treetops mingling with the young man's straight, longish hair.

Fran flipped the book over and read the blurb. *The Heart of the Wild* was the story of a teenager who lost both his parents in a plane crash and retreated to live alone in the woods of Oregon. He was content to be a nineteen-year-old hermit until he was discovered by a young woman wandering aimlessly through the woods, mourning the recent death of her husband. They fell in love but, as the blurb said, it was a "painful, bittersweet romance."

She turned the book over and studied the sketch on the cover again. It looked a little like Paul.

"Hey, you ready to move on?"

Fran jumped, startled by the abrupt question.

Maggie was shifting her weight from one foot to the other, impatient to go. "You ready? It's getting too crowded in here," she complained.

"Okay," Fran said, her pounding heart beginning to calm down. "Just let me pay for this."

"What're you buying?"

"A book," Fran blurted, not really wanting to show it to Maggie.

"I can see that." Maggie grimaced. "But what book?"

"This!" Fran relented and held the paperback up in front of her face.

"Hmmm." Maggie took the book and examined the cover. "Cute guy," she commented.

Fran's heart thumped, fearing that Maggie would see the resemblance between the sketch and Paul Wingate.

Maggie handed it back to Fran. "Let me know if it's any good. Maybe I'll read it."

Fran let out her breath in relief. "You? Read a whole book? Are you feeling well?"

"Fran, I'm sorry for what happened downstairs. I promise I won't try to force you into things anymore, okay? Now, go pay for the book, please. I want to stop by Music Towne before lunch."

"Thanks, Mag. I need all the friends I can get." She rushed to the cashier, eager to get her book hidden in a paper bag.

The girls strolled down the brick sidewalks of Mount Auburn Street in order to avoid the crush on Massachusetts Avenue. Passing several restaurants, some Harvard dorms, and the odd, triangular, castlelike building that housed the offices of the *Harvard Lampoon*, Fran and Maggie wound their way to Bow Street, where Music Towne was located.

"I just have to stop in for a minute to give Fred my Social Security number," Maggie explained as they approached the record shop.

"Who's Fred?" Fran asked.

"He's the store manager. I had to fill out tax forms for him last week, but I forgot my Social Security card at home. I just have to fill in the number."

Then just as Maggie was about to enter Music Towne, she noticed that Fran wasn't behind her. She looked back and saw Fran staring across the street, frozen in her tracks.

Maggie turned and tried to see what she was looking at. She looked across the street. There was an office furniture store, a bike shop, and an outdoor café. The furniture store was empty. In front of the bike shop, a guy was tightening the chain on a bike for a little kid. About a dozen people sat eating lunch outside the café. Maggie looked back at Fran, who had turned away and was now surveying the scene in the reflection of Music Towne's plate-glass window. Maggie looked back across the street.

Aunt Jane must be at the café, Maggie figured. Why else would Fran freak out like this? Maggie scrutinized every person at the café, but there was no sign of their aunt. Then she checked out the bike shop again. The guy who had been crouched down behind the kid's bike was now standing. It was Paul Wingate.

Maggie stomped over to Fran. "Hey, what's your problem?" She was still puzzled by Fran's behavior.

"Nothing." Fran wouldn't turn around and face her sister.

"I don't get it. What's gotten into you?"

"Nothing, I said." Fran gritted her teeth. "Go in and do your business."

"Hey, there's no one over there! Just that cute guy from your class, Paul Wingate—" All of a sudden Maggie's face lit up like a Christmas tree. "I don't believe it!" she said in amazement. "I don't believe it! By any chance, does my dear sister have a crush on—Paul Wingate?"

"Shut up," Fran muttered.

"You do!" Maggie squealed gleefully. "You do have a crush on Paul! Wow!"

"Don't be ridiculous. I do not."

"Then why are you as pale as a ghost? And why are your hands shaking?" Maggie had a big, mischievous grin plastered across her face. "Hey, come on, Fran. You can tell me."

"*Leave me alone!*" Fran was crying.

Maggie's heart suddenly ached for her. Fran had a crush on Paul, and she had it bad. "Stop crying, Fran," she said soothingly, putting an arm around Fran's shoulder. "Dry your eyes so we can go in and finish my business with Fred. Then we'll go across the street and say hi to Paul."

"No!" Fran's eyes flashed, and she recoiled from Maggie.

"Look, I know I just said I wasn't going to push you into anything, but can I give you some advice, Fran?"

Fran didn't answer.

"I know how you feel, but hiding your emotions never does any good. And wanting someone but doing nothing about it is just plain stupid. If you think about a guy all the time, eventually he becomes like a god. Untouchable. I'll bet you've never even talked to him, have you?"

Fran shook her head in misery.

"I want you to try to talk to him. He's just another person. There's nothing to be afraid of."

"No—I can't—"

"See what I mean? You've made him unapproachable, and now you're miserable."

"But what if he—he—?"

"What? What could he do? I know him. He's a nice guy. I bet he'll be happy to see some Medford High kids."

"I don't know, Maggie."

"Don't worry about it. We'll go together. Come on." Maggie gave Fran a tissue to wipe

43

her eyes and blow her nose. She then pushed the hair out of Fran's face and led her across the street toward Cambridge Cycles.

Paul was crouched down behind another bike now, tightening the spokes on the front wheel. He didn't notice Fran and Maggie approaching him.

"Just be cool," Maggie whispered to Fran, who was stiff and nervous. "Hey, Paul!" Maggie called out brightly. "How ya doin'?"

Paul peered through the spokes, trying to locate the voice. "Oh, hi, Maggie, Fran. How ya doin'?" Paul had a deep voice that matched his calm, take-charge personality. When he stood up, Fran noticed again his strong, broad shoulders, longish dark hair, and ruddy complexion. And she realized again why so many girls in Medford High had wanted to date the elusive Paul Wingate. True, he was the quiet type, but when he spoke, people seemed to listen. Something about him commanded attention. "In the market for a bike?" he asked, looking at Fran.

Fran froze, a bolt of panic shooting through her stomach. "No," she blurted, then hated the abrupt way she sounded.

"No, we're here on other business," Maggie quickly cut in. "I'm going to be working across the street at Music Towne. I have to fill out some tax forms today."

"Hey, great." Paul smiled warmly. "It'll be

nice having a friendly face from Medford High just across the street. How about you, Fran? You working this summer?"

"Ah—well, maybe," she said haltingly, looking down at the bike. "I mean, I may be working at the *Boston Globe* in August. But I'm enrolled in summer school right now. But that may not last . . . ."

"What are you taking in summer school?" Paul seemed to be genuinely interested, and this made Fran even more nervous.

"Well, ah—it's this special Harvard program for—ah, getting into college early." It was torture for Fran to have to reveal this.

"So you're planning on starting college in September?" Paul looked interested, but Fran decided he was just being polite.

"No, no—I don't plan on staying with the program. No, I'll be back at Medford High in the fall." Fran spoke rapidly, desperately wanting Paul to understand that she wasn't the hopeless brain he probably thought she was.

"You know, I thought of applying for that program myself, but I decided I didn't want to miss my senior year. Not that I'd necessarily have gotten in."

He looked over his shoulder just then. A little boy and his father were examining a bike, and the father was looking around for a salesman.

"Oh-oh, I'd better get back to work," Paul said calmly. "Look, as long as you both are going to be around the square, why don't you stop by sometime, and we can have lunch or something?" Paul's offer was made easily and offhandedly, but Fran was still speechless from what he'd said earlier about almost having applied for the summer school program. She wouldn't have thought someone like Paul would have actually *chosen* to attend a gifted program.

"Great," Maggie said enthusiastically. "We will."

"So I'll be seeing you two around, okay? Let me take care of these people before I lose a sale. Bye now."

"So long, Paul." Maggie smiled.

"Bye," Fran practically whispered.

As they walked back across Bow Street, heading for Music Towne, Maggie was beaming. "This is great, Fran! He's really a nice guy, isn't he? Perfect for you. I see good things in your future."

"Yeah." But Fran really wasn't listening. Now she had a real problem, and she could feel a headache coming on because of it. The more she thought about it, the more her temples throbbed. She didn't want to go to this summer school, but it would give her the opportunity to be in Harvard Square all summer. The perfect situation for getting close to Paul, she thought.

But then if she completed the special program, she would have to start college in September. In other words no senior year and no Paul. And then there was the possibility of working in downtown Boston at the *Globe* and, of course, her aunt's probable overreaction to all of this. All of a sudden Fran was more frantic and confused than Harvard Square rush-hour traffic.

Chapter 4

On Monday morning at quarter to nine, Maggie and Fran stood waiting for the Harvard Square bus. Fran was wearing her denim skirt, Mexican peasant blouse, and flat sandals. Maggie had on her tightest jeans, a zebra-stripe T-shirt, and high-heeled clogs.

"I'm sure glad I start work today," Maggie grumbled. "Another minute with *your* aunt and I might have done something drastic."

"Don't give her to me," Fran said. "She's your aunt, too."

"Yeah, I know. And a real pain in the—"

"I know, I know." Fran nodded sympathetically.

"I mean, first she makes us do the dishes by hand because she doesn't like the way the

49

dishwasher does them. Then she won't let us watch *Gone With the Wind* on TV, says it's 'trash,' and puts on some stupid documentary about Iceland. Who cares about Iceland?"

"She does, of course. It fits her personality."

"Yeah, cold. Do you know she actually told me I should put on a dress for work? Couldn't you just see me in a skirt at Music Towne? They'd fire me on the spot!"

"At least you get to escape and have some fun at work. I have to go to this retarded summer program. I know I'll hate it. I don't even know why I'm going." Fran sighed deeply, totally frustrated with her predicament.

"Well, at least you know it's only temporary. When Dad comes home, Aunt Jane and her summer school can take a walk." Maggie impatiently fingered a lock of her curly black hair. "Where's the bus? We're going to be late."

"I'm in no hurry," Fran said sadly. She was still wracking her brain for a way she could see Paul in the square without going to summer school and without having her aunt find out. Of course, Fran wouldn't discuss her problem with Maggie. She knew what Maggie would say— grab Paul, then quit summer school. Well, Fran knew that might be easy for Maggie to do, but it certainly wasn't for her. She couldn't just come on strong to Paul. What if he rejected her? No, Fran knew she had to go slowly. First, she had to start up a good friendship with Paul, something she had wanted to do since last winter when she had started noticing him. Then wait and see how things developed. You had to be careful with this sort of thing, Fran felt, especially with a boy like Paul. You had to be very careful with love. Maggie treated it like making scrambled eggs, but Fran was convinced that true love was really like creating a soufflé. She started wondering again if Paul was really an intellectual and, if so, why he didn't seem the type.

But by now the bus had come, reminding Fran that she had a more immediate problem to face. All the way to Harvard Square she tried not to worry about it, but the first-day-of-school butterflies were getting the better of her. She tried thinking of Paul, but that only made her feel worse, realizing how complicated her situation was. All she could think of was a seesaw: Paul and summer school were on one side, and the *Globe* apprenticeship and no Paul were on the other. It seemed that the only way she could be near Paul was to be in the square all the time, and the only way she could do that was by staying with the summer school.

"So are you going to the bike shop to see him today?" Maggie asked eagerly.

"Maggie! It's only the first day. It will look so obvious."

"Fran!" Maggie's tone was scolding.

"Well, I'll try—if I have time—maybe . . ."

*   *   *

A half-hour later Fran was wandering through Harvard Yard, looking for Emerson Hall, and for the moment Paul became the second biggest thing on her mind. The knots in her stomach tightened as she imagined just how dreadful this advanced summer school program could be.

Although Fran had been to Harvard Square countless times, she had never really explored the university itself. It was much bigger than she had expected, with large rectangular lawns separating each of the many old buildings. She considered asking one of the university students for directions, but they all looked so intense and distracted—walking along the brick paths with their heads down, leaning forward as if walking into a strong wind—that Fran was afraid to disturb any of them. But it was only twenty minutes to nine, so Fran figured she still had time to find Emerson Hall on her own.

She continued to wander, but soon she realized that trying to locate one ivy-covered brick building among dozens of similar buildings was futile without directions. Fortunately she spotted a campus policeman standing on the steps of a dormitory, drinking coffee from a paper cup.

"Sir? Excuse me, but could you tell me where Emerson Hall is?"

He pointed to a large, gray, marble building

with huge columns and a long flight of steps in front. "Do you see Widner Library over there?"

"The one with all the steps?" Fran nodded.

"Right. Walk toward it, then take a left on the path. Emerson will be the second building on your right."

"Thanks."

"Sure thing." He smiled, then returned to his coffee.

As she walked toward the imposing façade of Widner Library, she remembered her aunt saying that it was the only good library in the area and that a Widner Library card was better than an American Express card. It didn't exactly look like a fun place to Fran, but of course her aunt never allowed herself to have fun. Still, Fran was more than a little curious to check it out for herself. Maybe later, she thought as she walked past it.

The first building on her right must have housed the foreign language departments because when Fran looked in on the basement level classrooms, she could see a lot of students wearing headphones and mouthing words. It was obviously a language lab.

The next building was Emerson Hall, a dark, three-story building shaped like a single giant brick. Fran stopped on the front steps and sighed. She looked back at the lush lawn and the flowering bushes.

This is summer—what am I doing here? I don't want more school!

But then the reasons came back to her—the desire to be in Harvard Square near Paul, and the fear of her aunt's criticism. And she could always get out of it—her father had promised that she could quit if she didn't like it.

"Okay. I'll stick it out until Dad gets back," she whispered to herself. "I'll keep an open mind and hope for the best. Then when Dad comes home, I'll decide what I'm going to do." She started to climb the front steps. "Maybe Paul will ask me to run away with him in the meantime," she muttered under her breath.

Taking a deep breath, Fran pushed through the heavy glass door and was immediately surprised to see that such a somber place as Emerson Hall had pale, tangerine-colored walls. What seemed even sillier to her was the massive, muddy brown metal statue of Ralph Waldo Emerson sitting by the front door. Fran stopped for a moment and examined his dour face with its grim, determined chin and furrowed brow.

"How would you like to meet my aunt?" Fran muttered.

Fran left Ralph and went off to find Room 117, where the program would have most of its classes. There would be twenty-two students, and they would all take advanced math and English composition together in Room 117 in the mornings. In the afternoons the group would

54

split up into three sections—science, social sciences, and humanities, and students would get a basic knowledge of the various fields in these individual areas. The students got to choose whichever group they wanted, and Fran had already picked social sciences. And although she didn't want to admit it, the prospects of this part of the program did seem pretty interesting, promising to cover American, European, and world history, psychology, sociology, and some law.

Fran walked slowly down the long corridor, looking at the numbers on all the doors she passed. Finally she found 117, the second to the last on the right. The room was painted sea green. Through the large windows Fran could see an imposing wrought-iron, spiked fence and traffic beyond it. It was just like prison, she thought.

Crossing the threshold, she took her first look at her fellow students and instantly wanted to turn and leave for good. At the back of the room, three boys were huddled together, each one furiously punching figures into his pocket calculator. Two girls, both wearing glasses, and a fat boy sat in the front row, each silently bent over a book. Fran's heart sank at the sight of so many brains in one room. She didn't look like that—did she?

Then she spotted a tiny redhead staring out the window. She was wearing jeans, high-heeled sandals, and a tube top. Her hair was short and curly like Maggie's. Fran walked toward her, hoping to make friends with the only normal-looking kid in the class. But before Fran could even think of something to say, the redhead barked, "Hi. My name is Donna Ramsey. I'm one sixty-eight. What are you?" She had a voice like a machine gun.

"Pardon me?" Fran forced herself to smile and tried not to look as if anything was wrong.

"I said, I'm one sixty-eight. What about you?" Donna was agitated and impatient.

"Sorry, but I don't know what—"

"Your IQ," Donna interrupted. "What's your IQ?"

"I—I don't know," Fran lied and shrugged.

"How could you not know?" she demanded. "You see that girl over there? She's only one forty-seven. One forty-seven! They promised my mother that no one under one fifty would get into this program. And I'll bet she's not the only one. I mean, it's not fair to the rest of us. They'll just hold us back. Well, I'm not staying here. No sir, not until they weed out the slow kids." And with that she turned and shot out of the room.

Fran just stared at her departure in disbelief. "And they call that gifted," she muttered.

It was as bad as she had suspected it would be, and class hadn't even started yet. Fran stared out the window, letting her depression envelop her. Then she realized what she was staring at. Beyond the iron fence and the rushing traffic was Bow Street. She could make out the blue neon sign in the Music Towne window and the row of ten-speeds on the sidewalk in front of Cambridge Cycles.

Maggie and Paul were out there, she thought longingly, wishing she could be out there with them, working at a summer job like a normal kid. Squinting out the window, hoping to catch a glimpse of Paul, Fran felt like a real prisoner now.

Rescue me, Paul! Rescue me! she called out in her mind.

"Hello."

Fran jumped. The voice seemed to be right behind her head. She looked over her shoulder quickly.

The boy standing behind her was wearing a neatly pressed seersucker suit, crisply starched white shirt, and a red-and-blue striped tie. His hair was longish, straight, and black; his complexion was dark. He had big, sad eyes and a nice smile.

"Hello. My name is Ajit—Ajit Bannerji."

"Oh—hi. I'm Fran—Pastore."

"I am very glad to know you, Fran." He offered her his hand. She shook it reluctantly, not really wanting to make friends with any of the heavy-duty brains, even though she had to

57

admit he was kind of cute and certainly much friendlier than nutty Donna Ramsey.

"Yes, nice to meet you. What did you say your name was?"

"A-jit Ban-ner-ji," he pronounced. "I was born in India, but my family moved to Cambridge when I was nine. My father is a physicist. He came to study at MIT."

"Oh." Fran didn't know how to respond to this kind of open confidence.

"Yes. I hope to be a doctor myself, even though my father doesn't exactly approve. You see, he is a man of hard science. Medicine is too humanistic and therefore unpredictable, he says."

"What's so unpredictable about being a doctor?" Fran asked.

"People, of course. Emotions and feelings get in the way of scientific fact, my father says. In a way he's right, don't you think?"

"Oh, I'm sure he is," Fran said vaguely.

"And what do you hope to do, Fran?"

Fran felt as if she were being put on the spot. The only intention she had right now was to get tight with Paul, a rather frivolous endeavor compared to Ajit Bannerji's goal.

"Me? Ah—I want to be a—warden. I want to run a prison." It was the first thing that crossed her mind. She hoped it was weird enough to scare him off.

"How interesting!" Ajit gushed. "I could tell

58

when I first saw you that you were an interesting person. How did you pick prison work?"

Oh, brother! How am I going to get rid of him?

"Well," Fran said, letting her imagination take over, "my father was the warden at Sing-Sing for over twenty years. I grew up there, used to play with the inmates when I was a kid. I really loved them. They're basically good people—I know it. Now I want to be a warden, too, so I can help them."

Ajit's eyes widened, and his mouth hung open. "Fascinating!"

"Not really, Ajit. Living in a prison is like having a very big family, that's all. A family in need."

"Yes. I suppose so."

Fran almost burst out laughing. The more he swallowed of her story, the more she wanted to feed him. She began to feel guilty about leading him on like this, but she was enjoying it too much to stop.

"You're very interesting, Fran. I'd like to discuss your childhood further after class if you don't mind."

"Ah—well—you have to excuse me now, Ajit. I always meditate before class, and there're only a few minutes left." Fran abruptly plopped down into a seat, slapped her hands flat on the desktop, and shut her eyes.

Enthralled with his new acquaintance, Ajit

took the desk next to hers and watched her closely. "I've never meditated myself," he whispered, amazed to see a Western teenager practicing an Eastern tradition.

Sitting stiff with her eyes shut tight, Fran felt ridiculous. She wished she could disappear or at least levitate herself out the window. How could she have told him all that stuff? That was something Maggie would have done.

Just then the teacher whisked into the room, a tall, skinny man with a bushy handlebar mustache, a big grin, and tiny eyes hiding behind thick, wire-rim glasses. He was casually dressed in worn tan cords and a denim shirt open at the collar, the sleeves rolled up to his elbows.

"Good morning," he said in a gentle baritone. "I'm Sam Patel, your math instructor."

Fran's eyes shot open instantly at the sound of his voice, and she scrabbled for her pen and notebook in her bag. Opening her notebook to a blank page, she could see out of the corner of her eye that Ajit was still staring at her. She tried to ignore him.

Chapter 5

Maggie held her cup poised before her lips, but the frown on her face wasn't for the breakfast coffee. She glared at Fran, who was carefully buttering her English muffin to avoid eye contact with her sister. Once again, Fran's unruly hair was partially covering her face, hiding her from Maggie's disappointment.

"Sometimes you can be very aggravating. Do you realize that, Fran?" Maggie's tone was slow and serious, which was worse than screaming hysteria, Fran felt. It was clear that Maggie was really upset with her.

"Maggie," Fran started to whine, "I told you last night—class ran late Monday and yesterday. I didn't have a chance to go over to see Paul."

"Come on, Fran. Admit it. You got cold feet. You chickened out."

"Noooo. I—just haven't had time."

"Will you go see him today?"

"Sure—if I get out of class early enough."

"See! You're already making excuses. You have no intention of doing anything."

"That's not true! I want to see Paul, you know that, but—"

"But what?" Maggie snapped.

"But I'm not you!" Fran yelled. "I've got to do this my way. I have to take things slow." There were tears in her eyes.

Maggie sighed. "I'm sorry. I keep forgetting that this is all new to you. Sometimes you seem like you're stuck in neutral, and I want to give you a little push."

"I don't want a push! Oh, why is this all so hard for me?" Fran sobbed in frustration.

"Stop crying, Fran. You make it sound like you're the only one in the world who's ever gone through this. Everybody feels like this when they're in love. Not just you."

Fran was shocked that her sister was able to just blurt out love like that. The word was too precious to be used so casually, she felt.

"I think you're taking this a little too seriously. I mean, this isn't *Wuthering Heights* or *Dallas* or anything like that. He's a nice guy, you're a nice girl, and you two should be together. It's as simple as that."

"Oh, you make it sound so simple. What am I supposed to do? Walk into the bike shop and say, 'Paul, you're a nice guy, I'm a nice girl, we should be going together'? Is that how it's done?"

"Well, you'll never get anywhere if you run away from him."

"I am not running away from him!"

"Then go visit him today. If he likes you, he'll take care of the rest. Trust me."

"Ha!" Fran bit into her English muffin as if she wanted to hurt it. Maggie always had an answer for her, always. Fran really did want to go over to Cambridge Cycles, but after six hours cooped up with the superbrains, she had been depressed and cranky both days, unable to cope with romantic maneuvers. The classes went from bad to worse, and even the social studies group in the afternoon was little consolation. The material that would be covered in the section was intriguing, but Ms. Goostray, the instructor, wasn't. And the superbrains were already driving her crazy. She spent the better part of each afternoon trying to reassure herself that even if she was smart, she wasn't like them. However, despite Ms. Goostray and the brains, there was one good thing about the social studies class. Ajit Bannerji wasn't in it.

Ajit just wouldn't give up, and she didn't know how to get rid of him without hurting his feelings.

63

He didn't seem like a bad guy, but he was much too eager, especially when Fran was quietly brooding over Paul.

Sitting at the kitchen table, Fran was just about to sink into despair over her situation when Maggie nudged her and glanced toward the back door. Heavy footsteps could be heard pounding up the wooden stairs, about to enter the kitchen. Instantly the girls sat up straight and concentrated on their breakfasts.

The back door swung open, and Jane bounced in, wearing her red running shorts, worn Adidas, and Boston Marathon T-shirt. "Good morning," she chirped.

"Morning."

"Good morning."

The sisters exchanged stealthy looks over the rims of their coffee cups as their aunt went about her morning ritual.

Still pumping her knees and working her feet into the linoleum, running in place, Jane got five oranges out of the refrigerator, sliced them in half, then mauled them in the electric juicer she'd brought over from her apartment. The juicer was as efficient as she was, and the sound it made was almost painful.

"There's some orange juice already made in the refrigerator," Maggie interjected just as the third half-orange was about to be sacrificed.

"Not *fresh* orange juice, Margaret."

The brutal sacrifice continued, and Maggie rolled her eyes to the ceiling like Groucho Marx. Fran had to bite the insides of her cheeks to keep from laughing out loud.

When the juicer had finally produced a tall glass of orange juice, Jane then took a cereal bowl down from the cupboard and took her shoebox out of the refrigerator. The box contained all her vitamin bottles—the entire alphabet from A to Zinc. Still running in place, she methodically opened each bottle and placed a pill in the bowl. By the time she finally sat down to have her "breakfast," Fran and Maggie's stomachs were aching with suppressed laughter.

"Is that all you're having for breakfast again?" Maggie asked as her aunt systematically put one pill on her tongue, washed it down with a sip of juice, then took the next pill in the same measured way.

"It's all anyone really needs," Jane announced confidently. "Anyway I'm having lunch out today. This will offset whatever sins I commit at the Blue Parrot."

"The Blue Parrot?" Maggie commented. "Have the Monte Cristo sandwich—it's really great."

"I never eat anything that's fried. No one should. Deadly for the heart.

"By the way, you two are welcome to join me. I'm having lunch with Janet Drew, Frances, my friend who teaches in your program."

"Oh, yeah. She's the science instructor. I don't have her."

"Too bad. She's a very bright woman. I think you'd enjoy getting to know her."

Fran thought for a minute. Anything that involved her aunt and her friends was sure to be dull. But at least she'd have an excuse if Ajit asked to have lunch with her. Consoling herself with the fact that the Blue Parrot was a very pleasant restaurant, Fran agreed to meet her aunt for lunch.

"And you, Margaret? Will you join us?" Aunt Jane asked.

"I'm afraid I can't. I only get a half-hour for lunch." Thankfully, Maggie added mentally. Then she glanced sharply at Fran, and Fran knew exactly what she was thinking.

Why don't you go to the bike shop for your lunch break instead?

Fran's big brown eyes glistened with quiet anxiety and desperation. Fran couldn't bear more scolding from her sister. She felt as if she were being pulled in all directions, and now Maggie was pulling hardest. "Maybe I'll stop by Music Towne after class today, Maggie. Is that okay with you?"

"Sure. Please do. *We'll* be glad to see you." Maggie eyed her sister suspiciously.

In the meantime Jane continued to take her vitamins, one at a time, oblivious to everything else.

* * *

Fran's third day of classes was awful. The first half of the morning was tolerable because Mr. Patel, the math instructor, was a pretty decent guy. Unfortunately, math did not move Fran's soul the way it did most of the other students in her class, so she couldn't really say she was enjoying it.

Fran admired Mr. Patel because he treated the group as though they were plain old students, which was just what they were, Fran felt. Just because they learned faster didn't mean they already knew everything, and Mr. Patel made sure they kept that fact in mind.

But then there was Mrs. Lowell, the English instructor. She was obviously in awe of the superbrains because she let them run her class. Tiny and frail with long wheat-blond hair and a toothy smile, Mrs. Lowell encouraged all the superbrains' bad habits, and this infuriated Fran. Rather than taking control of her class, Mrs. Lowell allowed her discussions to go off on tangents instigated by the students.

When Mrs. Lowell dismissed class for the morning, Fran was surprised to see Ajit dash out of class. He had impressed her as the hard to discourage type, and she had fully expected him to throw himself at her, begging to have lunch with her again. She could have sworn that he was dying to talk to her from the way he was

67

looking at her before class ended. Maybe he had gotten the message that she wasn't interested.

Fran gathered up her notebook and shoulder bag and went out into the tangerine hallways, on her way to meet her aunt and her aunt's friend Janet Drew at the Blue Parrot. It was too bad she had agreed to go to this lunch, she thought, because Ajit hadn't bothered her after all. Well, at least the food would be good.

As she passed the statue of Emerson by the front doors, Fran looked up into his dour face. "The perfect match for my aunt." She shook her head and sighed. "Why don't you go to this lunch in my place?"

Emerson refused to commit himself, though, so Fran went on her way.

Rather than cut through Harvard Yard, Fran decided to go by way of Massachusetts Avenue. As soon as she emerged from the tranquil campus onto the bustling square, Fran strained to see the bicycles lined up outside Cambridge Cycles on the far side of the intersection. She thought of Paul and her promise to Maggie that she would go over to see him today, and suddenly the butterflies started fluttering in her stomach. Then, through the rushing traffic, she saw him. He was carrying a bike out of the shop. The bike was hoisted up on one shoulder, and he was holding it with one hand. Fran was overwhelmed by the mere sight of him. He seemed so wonderful to her she could have burst into tears right there on the corner of Quincy Street and Massachusetts Avenue.

I want to see Paul, I really do, but—

Fran glanced over at the blue neon Music Towne sign.

No buts. After social studies today, I'm going to do it.

Fran nodded to herself and suddenly felt dizzy with hope and expectations. Even lunch with her aunt—even her aunt at her very worst—couldn't dampen this wonderful feeling.

With wings on her feet, Fran wove through the crush of pedestrians, past the perennially busy Coop, past all the little shops on Mount Auburn Street, to the other end of Harvard Square, where the small restaurant was nestled behind the courtyard of an early nineteenth-century clapboard guest house. Fran flew into the Blue Parrot, looking forward to a big salad of some kind and a tall iced tea. Standing by the bar, she gazed around the room, peering through the many spindly spider plants that hung from the ceiling. Then she spotted her aunt waving to her from the back of the restaurant. Fran approached the table with a delirious grin, which seemed to surprise even Jane, who generally never noticed whether people were happy or not. But when Fran suddenly saw who was seated at the table with the two women, her bright grin withered, like a flower in a heat wave, to a look of dismay.

"Frances," Jane announced, giving her a prissy little smile. "I want you to meet Janet Drew and Ajit Bannerji, her star pupil from Cambridge Latin High, where she teaches during the year."

If an earthquake had opened up a hole in the floor at that moment, Fran would have jumped in without hesitating.

"Oh, Ms. Harrigan! This is your niece?!" Ajit exclaimed, the delirious grin now on *his* face. "Why, we've already met! Haven't we, Fran?"

"Er—ah, yes. This is a surprise, Ajit."

"I'm pleased to meet you, Frances," Janet Drew cut in. She squinted at Fran from behind her thick glasses.

"Hello, Ms. Drew." Fran was amazed at how similar Janet Drew was to her aunt. They were almost replicas of one another, except that Janet was a brunette and Jane was a blond. *Just like salt and pepper shakers,* Fran thought as she tried to force a pleasant smile.

"Well, I'm glad to see that you two found each other," Janet commented. "From what your aunt tells me, Frances, you and Ajit share many intellectual interests."

"Yes." Ajit's eyes were wide with enthusiasm. "I didn't know you liked classical music too, Fran."

Oh, no! Don't mention that business about growing up in Sing-Sing and wanting to be a warden and all that! Or the meditation before class, either.

"Ms. Drew, did you know that Fran wants to be a prison warden?" Ajit announced. "I think that's great."

"What?" Jane leaned forward.

No, Ajit!

"Yes, Fran told me that she wants to follow in her father's footsteps and help poor misguided souls like the ones in her big family back at Sing-Sing."

"What is this all about, Frances?" Jane demanded, a steely edge to her voice.

"Oh, ah—well, ah, that was a joke, Ajit." Fran could feel the perspiration gathering in her armpits. "Oh, I guess you haven't heard about the prison jokes—everybody's telling them."

Jane and Janet stared blankly at Fran, the light glinting off their glasses.

"You know—like there used to be chicken jokes and pickle jokes. Well, now there are prison jokes. . . ." Fran felt as if she were talking a foreign language. The three of them looked at her as if she had just landed from the moon. Gradually Fran's curtain of hair began to creep forward to cover her embarrassment.

"Frankly, I've never felt that this type of

71

humor contributed anything to modern civilization," Janet declared snippily.

"I agree," Jane snapped. "Really, Frances, I don't know why someone with your intelligence finds this kind of low-life culture so amusing."

Fran's heart was pounding. She wanted to start breaking plates, screaming, anything to vent her anger. Instead, she sat motionless, her chest heaving.

"Oh, but I disagree, Ms. Harrigan," Ajit protested, giving a strange but infectious giggle. "Jokes are always very important to a society. Freud himself said that. And even Abraham Lincoln loved jokes. He published several volumes of joke books."

"Well—yes, that's true, Ajit." Jane was perturbed by Ajit's unexpected defense, and she wasn't used to being challenged. "Of course, there are jokes, and then there are jokes," she added lamely.

"But you have to admit, only time can judge their individual value." Grinning confidently, Ajit would not budge from his position.

"Ah—yes, that's correct." In the face of a strong argument from Ajit and in the presence of his mentor, her own best friend, Jane conceded.

Fran couldn't believe it. She had never seen her aunt back down like this. Pushing the hair out of her face, Fran smiled despite herself. Ajit was a superbrain, but he was still okay. Fran would have to thank him after lunch.

"Well, shall we order?" Fran finally suggested, giving a tiny grin of satisfaction.

Chapter 6

"So, how was lunch?" Maggie asked casually that night.

"Awful! That guy Ajit was there. It turns out he's the star pupil of Aunt Jane's friend."

"Oh, brother, and you thought you were getting away from him."

"Right, and now he's more persistent than ever. I'm afraid to say it, but I think he likes me a lot."

"So? Why didn't you just tell him he's a nice guy, but you're interested in someone else?"

"I couldn't say that!" Fran's face started to get hot. She knew Maggie was about to start nagging her about Paul.

"Why not? I would."

"I know *you* would but—I don't know. I

wouldn't feel right." Fran flushed at the thought of being so outspoken with a boy.

"Anyway, what happened after that?"

"He went to his science section, I went to my social studies section, and I didn't really think about him after that. As a matter of fact, I wasn't paying very much attention to class, either, because all I could think about was Paul and how I was finally going to go over to the bike shop after class."

"Come on, Fran. Don't give me that. You promised me you'd come to the store this afternoon, and you never showed up."

Fran couldn't look at her sister. "Well, I *was* thinking about him," she said defensively. "But I—uh—" Her voice faltered as she tried to think of an excuse Maggie would buy. The truth was that the closer it had come to school letting out, the more panicked Fran had felt. After school, she had stood across the street from the bicycle shop, waiting for Paul to come out. Maybe, she thought, she could just casually walk by and say hi. But Paul had not appeared, and Fran couldn't think of any excuse for going into the store. So she had gone home.

"Well, listen, sister, you'd better stop thinking about him and start doing something, that's all I have to say. Follow me."

Fran wouldn't budge. "Where are you going?"

"Don't be so suspicious. Trust me. I'm your sister."

Reluctantly Fran got to her feet, and Maggie immediately grabbed her elbow, leading her downstairs.

"Where are we going?" Fran demanded. "It's eight o'clock. Aunt Jane won't let us go out now."

"We're not going out." Maggie refused to elaborate.

They descended the staircase and rushed by the front parlor, where Aunt Jane was reading. "Frances! Margaret!" she called out as soon as she spotted them. "Where are you going?"

Maggie stopped dead in her tracks, jerking Fran to a halt, and grumbled something under her breath. She pulled Fran back and poked their heads into the parlor.

"Dad wanted us to straighten out the garage while he's away," Maggie said. "We want to get started before it gets dark."

"Oh, all right. Go ahead."

Aunt Jane returned to her book, and Maggie proceeded to guide Fran through the kitchen and out the back door to the detached one-car garage behind the house.

The garage was an old structure with a high roof and barn doors that creaked on their hinges. Jack Pastore had never put his car in it because it was so narrow, and the garage had become a dusty storage space for all kinds of things.

Maggie dug her keys out of her pocket and

unlocked the padlock, then swung open one of the doors.

"What are we doing here?" Fran huffed in exasperation. "What do you want in here?"

"Where's the light switch?" Maggie asked, ignoring her question.

"Over there." Fran pointed to the righthand corner.

Maggie groped in the dim corner, feeling for the switch. "There," she said as the naked bulb in the ceiling illuminated the small mountain of junk.

"Maggie, I still don't understand what we're going to find in here that's so important."

"If I told you what I'm looking for, you'd start crabbing at me again. So just sit still until I find it." Maggie turned and started moving cardboard boxes and snow tires and old lawn furniture, looking for the mysterious item.

Fran scowled, annoyed that her sister was treating her like she was helpless. After all, she was the older one, she shouldn't have to take this from Maggie. Fran turned away abruptly and stared moodily at the other end of the junk pile, where a dust-covered, navy blue-and-white baby stroller was parked against the wall.

Fran recalled a photograph that was pasted in one of the photo albums on the bottom shelf of the parlor bookcase. In that picture, she, as a toddler, was reaching up to push eighteen-month-old Maggie in that stroller. They were wearing identical sunsuits, bright yellow ones, and sun hats that looked like upside-down petunias. Maggie's dark hair was curling up under the brim of her hat, while Fran's straight bangs formed a fringe over her eyebrows. Fran loved that picture, but she had forgotten that the stroller was still around. She looked over at Maggie busily burrowing into the clutter and realized that in some ways Maggie had changed very little. She had always been the hardheaded, stubborn one. Once she set her sights on something, she didn't give up until she got what she wanted.

On the floor behind the stroller sat the beige plastic cat box that used to be Sweet Pea's. Looking at that cat box, Fran could picture Sweet Pea exactly, as if she were still around: a mischievous gray-and-white fur ball with big hazel eyes and huge ears.

That kitten had been so much fun, Fran thought. Too bad she had run away in a rainstorm.

Fran had cried and cried after Sweet Pea was gone. Maggie hadn't cried as much, Fran seemed to remember. When it became obvious that Sweet Pea wasn't coming back, Jane had taken Fran and Maggie aside and tried to console them.

She wasn't so sour back then, Fran recalled. *Always prim and proper, but it seems she was nicer then.*

Jane had told them that her fiancé's cat was pregnant and they could surely have a kitten from her litter. They never got another kitten, though. Aunt Jane's fiancé broke up their engagement before his cat had her kittens.

She never really had a boyfriend after him. I never really thought about it. Sad . . .

Suddenly a tremendous crash from within the junk pile jarred Fran from her memories.

"Well, have you found it yet?" Fran called out, expecting to disapprove of whatever *it* was.

"What?" The disembodied voice came from somewhere within the junk pile.

"I said have you found it yet?"

"*What?*" the voice demanded.

"Whatever it is you're looking for?" Fran was annoyed now.

"Yes! Why don't you help me get it out instead of just standing around?"

"*You* told me to sit still!"

"Just get over here and help me, will you?"

Fran glared into the corridor that Maggie had cleared for herself. At the end of it, Maggie was struggling to free her old bike, trying to set it upright so she could wheel it out.

"What do you want me to do?" Fran called out.

Maggie didn't answer, tugging harder until the bike was finally upright. "Here," Maggie grunted, "you grab the handlebars while I push." She straddled the back wheel and started to guide it through the narrow passageway. Fran reached in to pull, and soon they had Maggie's old bike out of the pile. They stood looking at it.

"What a mess!" Fran said, wrinkling her nose. "What were you going to do with this?"

"Me? Nothing." Maggie slapped the dust from her jeans. "It's for you."

"What am I supposed to do with it?" she asked coyly, even though she now had a pretty clear notion of what Maggie had in mind.

"What a dumbbell! You are going to take this to Cambridge Cycles to be repaired. That way you'll have a legitimate excuse for going to see Paul. Get it?"

"And how am I supposed to get it to Harvard Square?" Fran asked testily.

"You ride it!"

"How? The tires are flat, and the chain is rusty!"

"Well, then we'll put air in the tires. Don't worry about the chain, it'll get you to the bike shop."

"And who's going to pay for this—this overhaul?"

"Don't worry about it. I've got money."

"I'm touched by your generosity, but this scheme is like something out of *I Love Lucy*. It won't work." Fran crossed her arms over her chest.

"Then you're going to go into the bike shop

on your own tomorrow to talk to Paul and get him to take you out?"

"Well, ah—no—I can't—" Fran stumbled.

"Then I guess you need this old wreck. Here!" Maggie pushed the bike toward Fran, who caught it reluctantly.

"Oooh!" Fran moaned. "You think this is a big joke. You think it's going to be easy."

"Let's not get into that again. The fact is that you like Paul, but you're too embarrassed to go flirt with him the way I would. So you need a reason to go to the bike shop, and here it is."

"But—"

Maggie wasn't listening to another excuse. She turned her back on Fran and went back into the junk pile.

"Maggie! Listen to me!" Fran was almost pleading.

Maggie came back out with a rag and an old bicycle pump, which she held out to Fran. "Here, start pumping."

Fran just looked at the pump, her eyes glistening with nervousness and fear.

"Do you want to be just a brain all your life?"

Instantly Fran shot her sister a dirty look. "You're so kind."

Then she snatched the pump out of Maggie's hand and went to work on the tires as

Maggie started to wipe some of the grime off the seat and frame. "This better work," Fran mumbled. "This just better work."

On Sunday night, Fran was still feeling good about Ajit's triumph over her aunt. Actually, it was the only thing she had to celebrate all that week. Jane had gone into an immediate snit after that lunch at the Blue Parrot, and she had hardly spoken to Fran and Maggie all week. Except when the telegram came.

Late Saturday afternoon a messenger arrived at the house with a telegram. Jane signed for it, and after reading it, she summoned the girls right away to tell them that their father had written to tell them that he would be in Ireland for another week. Fran's face registered her deep disappointment—this meant she'd have to stay with that dreadful summer school for another week. At the time Fran thought it might have been her imagination, but her aunt seemed almost happy to hear that her brother-in-law's return would be delayed. She knew her aunt could be awful, but she refused to believe she was that bad. Still, her reaction continued to puzzle Fran.

Chapter 7

"Where are you going so early?" Jane asked Fran between vitamin pills the next morning.

"Ah—I'm taking Maggie's bike to school today. I decided I could, ah, use the exercise," Fran replied, inching toward the back door.

Maggie jumped in. "Yeah, we found my old three-speed in the garage last night, and Fran decided to start using it."

"I'm glad to see you're taking some interest in your health, Frances. You only get one body, you know, so you should treat it to some exercise on a regular basis."

"Yeah." Fran wasn't listening. Her mind was on getting the bike to Harvard Square and to Paul.

"You know, Margaret, it wouldn't hurt if

85

you did a little jogging or bicycling." Aunt Jane cast a judgmental eye at her younger niece.

"Are you kidding? I'm on my feet all day, dancing to the music at the store. You can't beat that for exercise."

"I'm sure I could," her aunt responded.

Fran had her hand on the doorknob now. "Well, so long. I'm off," she said, smiling weakly.

"Goodbye, Frances."

"Take it easy, Fran. And good luck with the bicycle." Maggie tried to suppress a sly grin.

"Thanks. I'll need it."

Fran left and closed the door behind her, clumping down the wooden steps. The old three-speed was locked to the railing where they had left it the night before. Fran sighed as she looked it over in the morning light, now having second thoughts about the whole scheme.

She turned to go back in, but then she thought of Maggie and what she would say. In all probability there would be a lecture on physical fitness from her aunt, too. Even if this bike caper was ridiculous, she thought, she had to give it a try.

She jumped down off the steps and dug into the deep pockets of her baggy off-white painter's overalls for the key to the lock. After removing the lock and securing it to the seat of the bike, Fran rolled up her pant legs, then mounted the three-speed, put up the kickstand with her heel, and pushed off.

The poor bike groaned, squeaked, and rattled, and Fran started to panic, fearing that it would collapse right under her. Could she really take this thing out onto Massachusetts Avenue? she wondered. She'd get killed in traffic.

She tried to pump harder, but the bike resisted her, creaking along at its own slow pace. Fran fiddled with the gearshift, but the three-speed did not respond. "This is going to be a long trip," she muttered.

As soon as she spotted the rush-hour traffic a block and a half away, she seriously considered turning back. She would never make it, she thought, afraid to attempt such a risky journey. But then the bike made the decision for her.

The old back tire couldn't hold air, and now it was perfectly flat. Fran pulled over, stared down at the tire, and bit her lip.

She could walk it home, then take the bus. But what about Paul? she thought. Failure again—damn! Of course, there was a gas station about two blocks away, over on Massachusetts Avenue. She could put air in the tire and just hope she could make it to the square.

Fran knew she'd hate herself later if she didn't try to get the bike into the bike shop and see Paul, so she hopped off and walked it to the Getty station, thinking that the tire probably had gone flat because she hadn't put enough air in it with the little hand pump. She pushed the bike to the station, past the gas pumps, to the air pump at the far end of the lot. The young attendant didn't even notice her, he was so busy tending to the commuters lined up for gas.

Fran rested the bike on the kickstand, then bent down to unscrew the valve cap and read the pressure limits on the tire. Maximum pressure—seventy pounds. Fran took the hose off the pump and cranked it to seventy, then carefully pressed the nozzle into the tire valve. The pump rang out four or five times as the tire got hard again, and then it stopped by itself. The tire looked full, so Fran coiled the hose and replaced it on its hook, then mounted the bike and went on her way.

Apprehensively she pulled out into the traffic, sweat forming on her forehead as she concentrated on keeping the bike on a steady course as far to the right as she could. The one thing that she dreaded most was the possibility that someone in one of the parked cars along the road would open his door in her path. Horrible visions of her swerving out into the roaring traffic or crashing into the open door filled her head.

But these fears faded fast because her tire went flat again. She had no other choice but to get off and walk it to the next gas station. Having only ridden about three or four blocks, now she had to walk it three more blocks to get more air.

"At this rate, I'll never make it," she grumbled to herself. "It's a good thing I left so early."

Fran stopped at the next gas station, located the air pump, and repeated the process of filling her bad tire. Unfortunately, three blocks later it was flat again, and she was forced to walk it to another air pump.

Cursing, she was more determined than ever to get to Cambridge Cycles that morning. She was only in Somerville now, halfway between Medford and Harvard Square, but she had reached the point of no return. It was only twenty minutes to nine, so she could probably walk it to the square in time to take the bike to Paul and still make class. Nevertheless, she had decided she was going to ride it in, and that's what she was going to do.

However, after stops for air at an Exxon station, a Shell station, an Amoco station, and a Mobil station, Fran gave up. When the tire went flat again just north of Harvard Square and she knew she'd have to go out of her way to get it filled, she decided to walk it through Harvard Yard to Bow Street.

It was almost nine-thirty now, and class started at ten.

Can I talk to Paul for that long? What am I going to say to him? Fran was panicking, but she kept on walking. Even though her brain had doubts and her stomach had butterflies, her feet kept going toward Cambridge Cycles. Despite all her fears and worries, at least she was finally going through with it.

Passing quickly along the brick paths that cut through the tranquil campus lawns, Fran wanted to get away from the university right away. If Ajit or Janet Drew suddenly popped out of the bushes, she knew she'd lose what little nerve she now had. This was no time for superbrain nonsense, she knew. This was a job for *superguts.*

She approached Emerson Hall and breezed through the imposing gates. Then standing on the red brick sidewalk, Fran peered across the avenue, through the river of rushing cars and buses, and saw him. Paul was setting up the new ten-speeds outside the bike shop. Fran froze. She had never expected to see him this soon. It wasn't fair, she thought, she should have had more time to prepare herself, to get psyched. But, no, the second she emerged from the sleepy, ivy-covered calm of Harvard, she was hit in the face with the raging traffic and choking exhaust and the sight of Paul.

She just stood there, watching him work. It was as if she were watching pioneer Paul tending to his chores across a white-water mountain river, separated from him by nature.

"Rescue me," she whispered, but the snarling traffic ground her soft plea into tiny pieces. She knew the only solution was for her to rescue herself. She had to go to him. Glancing up the street for oncoming cars, Fran took a deep breath and prepared to cross the perilous avenue.

As soon as there was a break in the traffic, Fran dashed across, forgetting about mountain rivers and pioneers, now concerned about making it across safely with the ungainly bike. Her heart was racing as she guided the squeaky, flat-tired bike to Cambridge Cycles. The cranky noises the old bike made were embarrassing, and she wanted to say "ssshh!" to it. She stood in front of the bike shop, frozen, wondering whether it was too late to back out.

This is dumb! He'll know right away that this is just a stunt. I know he will. He'll think I'm a real jerk. This'll never work out the way I want.

But it was too late. While she was lost in her thoughts, fretting over her situation, Paul spotted her from inside the shop, and now he was coming out.

Oh, no! What'll I say?!

"Hi, Fran," Paul said as he came through the open doorway. "How ya doin'?" His voice was low and easy, his manner very casual but not supercool.

"Oh—ah, hi, Paul!" Fran was about to melt in Paul's presence. "How are you this morning?" Fran hated the sound of her own voice. Everything she said sounded dumb to her.

"Pretty good, can't complain." He smiled. "Looks like you've got an ailing bike here." He looked down at the flat tire, then scrutinized the rest of it.

"Yeah, it's in pretty bad shape. We haven't used it in years. I—ah, wanted to do some serious riding this summer, so I thought I'd, you know, bring it to you for a checkup."

"Well, let's see." Paul stepped closer and started to examine the bike as Fran was still holding it up. Fran's fingers tingled on the handlebars as Paul tested the shift and the brakes, then stooped down to check out the chain and the tires. With Paul so close to her, she became a bit lightheaded and giddy. She liked the feeling.

"It needs a complete overhaul, Fran. New brake pads and new tires, too, I'm afraid. The rubber is beginning to dry-rot." He squeezed the flat tire and invited her to do the same. "See how it cracks? That's dry-rot."

Fran reached to feel the tire, and her hand brushed his shoulder. She practically fell over from jerking her hand away so violently. Then feeling the tire gingerly, Fran was careful not to touch him again, though she really wanted to.

"Do you think it's worth fixing?" she asked tentatively.

"Sure. I kinda like these old three-speeds

myself. I think they make pretty good touring bikes, although they'd never stand up in a race."

"I don't think I'll be doing much racing." She laughed shyly.

"Well, then I think it's worth fixing." Paul looked down at the ground and grinned self-consciously. "I don't mean to give you the hard sell or anything, but I'd do it if I were you."

"Well, you're the expert," she said, trying not to look at him intently. "Let's do it!" She felt her face flush—had she sounded as if she was coming on too strong?

Paul didn't seem to notice anything wrong with what she had said, however. "Okay, let's see." He scratched his head, estimating the amount of time he'd need to fix the bike. "Today is Monday—I can have it ready for you on Friday. Or do you need it sooner?"

"No, no, Friday is fine," she said, eager to be agreeable.

"I'm not positive, but the whole job will probably cost about fifty dollars."

"Okay." She nodded, then panicked as she suddenly realized that she didn't have anything else to say after they had exhausted the topic of the bike. "So, Paul, how do you like your summer job?" She knew it was a dumb question, but it would have to do.

"Oh, I really like it. Mr. Prince, the owner, is a pretty good boss. I mean, he doesn't hassle me or anything. And being in the square every day is a real trip."

"Yeah," she agreed. "I just wish I didn't have to be here going to summer school."

"I thought you said you were quitting that for a job at the *Globe* or something like that."

Fran's eyes widened with surprise and delight. He had remembered what she had told him the other day.

"Well, yeah. If everything works out, I'll be working at the *Globe* as a go-fer in August. I just hope I get it so I can get out of this summer school."

"Sounds like a great job, Fran. Too bad you won't be around the square, though." Paul looked down at the bike as he spoke.

"Yeah. Well, it hasn't happened yet. I may still be here all summer." Fran couldn't figure out his concern. It almost seemed as if he didn't want to see her go to work in Boston.

"Well, time will tell, I guess." He looked away again.

Fran was afraid to consider the possibility that maybe, just maybe, he felt something for her and that he was shyly hinting at wanting to see more of her. She didn't know what to say now.

"Ah, speaking of time"—she glanced at her watch—"I'd better get going if I'm going to make class on time."

"Oh."

She turned and started to walk away. "Bye, Paul."

"So long, Fran. See you on Friday, right?"

"Yeah, Friday. I'll be here."

"Good. It was nice to see you, Fran."

"Oh. Nice to see you too, Paul. Gotta run now. Bye."

"Uh, Fran," he suddenly said, "wait a minute. Can you, I mean would you like to meet me for lunch today?"

"Lunch. Well, sure, I'd love to. Where—I mean, should I meet you here? What time? My morning classes end at noon."

"Then I'll see you here at noon, okay? How does pizza sound to you?"

"Pizza sounds fantastic. See you then. Bye." Fran couldn't believe this was happening to her. She floated up Bow Street with wings on her heart and jet lifters on her feet. She could have flown, she was so deliriously happy.

At 12:05 Fran arrived at the bicycle shop and looked around nervously. She hoped she wasn't too late—or too early. Then she saw Paul heading her way.

"Hi, Fran. What perfect timing. I just finished cleaning up. Ever been to Pinocchio's?"

"Sure. I love their pizza."

"Then, let's go."

At Pinocchio's they both decided to live dangerously and ordered a large "super pie" with everything on it. Fran smiled nervously and hoped that their conversation that morning hadn't left them with nothing to talk about.

"So, Fran, what's it like?"

"What's what like?"

"Spending your summer surrounded by teenage geniuses."

"You really want to know?"

"Sure."

"I hate it. I mean, some of the kids are okay when you talk to them alone, but put them all together and everyone's always trying to outdo each other and intimidate the teachers with their superior brain power."

"So why don't you quit?"

"Well, I might—after this week. But my aunt did go to a lot of trouble to get me into this program."

"Aha, I had a feeling she might have been behind all this. You can't let her run your life, you know."

"She doesn't run my life," Fran said defensively.

"Oh, I'm sorry if I said something wrong. I don't mean to put the woman down. I just thought you might have a few gripes about her. She sort of got on me at the beginning of the year, always suggesting that I do extra work because I had a 'good head' for history. Finally, I had to tell her that history wasn't my subject. I told her I planned to be an engineer. She said

I was wasting my time and my intellect, but I just told her that I didn't think so. And she's left me alone ever since."

Fran looked at him in amazement. "I can't believe you said that to her," she breathed.

"What's her problem, anyway? You know, I feel kind of sorry for her. I figure there must be something missing from her own life if she has to be always pushing other people around and running their lives. I guess she thinks she's helping. Maybe she even thought she was helping Doug Flynn by embarrassing him all the time. Maybe she thought he'd get angry enough and start working harder. Anyway, that's when I first started thinking of you, when I talked to Doug on the last day of school. If she'd done such a number on Doug and me, I could just imagine what you were going through as her niece. That's why I was glad when you showed up at the shop the other day. I thought it might give us a chance to talk."

Suddenly the conversation didn't sound very romantic to Fran. She started to wonder if this was the only reason Paul had invited her to lunch. He just felt sorry for her, the way he had felt sorry for Doug Flynn. He wanted to help her cope with her aunt! Well, the last thing she needed today was to be treated like a charity case—and to spend her lunch hour talking about her aunt. Besides, who did he think he was, thinking he had her aunt all figured out?

Although Fran had to admit that he seemed to have done a good job of it. And he had given her aunt more credit than she herself ever had.

"Gee, Paul, here comes our pizza already. Say, have you seen any other kids from school at the bike shop this summer?"

Paul looked hurt that Fran had changed the subject, but Fran couldn't help herself. She was sure now that Paul was only interested in her as someone to be kind to, not as a girlfriend. How could she have misunderstood? Why would a popular boy like Paul be really interested in her? She rushed through her pizza and then left, saying she had to finish up a homework assignment before her next class. Then she ran to the door, so no one in Pinocchio's would see her tears.

Chapter 8

"If there are no further questions," Ms. Goostray droned, pausing for any last raised hands, "then class is dismissed."

Fran could barely pick her head up off her fist. Two hours with Ms. Goostray was torture. Pure, unadulterated boredom, to be precise. Fran admitted that it was hard for her to pay attention to anything after what had happened at lunch, but a class with Ms. Goostray was like a two-week vacation in a padded cell. With her sleepy eyelids and her slack-jawed monotone, Ms. Goostray simply could not make anything interesting, no matter what she was lecturing about.

Fran couldn't understand how the other students managed to stay attentive and apparently interested all day long, regardless of how dull the class was.

When class finally ended, Fran gathered up her books, eager to leave. She didn't want to have to talk to anyone, especially not Ajit.

She rushed through the doorway, but there was Ajit, lurking in the tangerine hallways, anxious to waylay her.

"Hello, Fran," Ajit called out hopefully. "How was your social science class?"

"Awful," Fran grumbled, sizing up just how difficult it would be to get rid of him this time. Considering that class was over for the day and he had no place in particular to go, Fran figured he'd be nearly impossible to lose.

Ajit trailed after her, desperately trying to keep up a conversation. Finally Fran turned to him and said, "Ajit, would you mind just leaving me alone right now? I've got a lot on my mind, and I just don't want to talk to anyone right now."

"Okay, Fran, I'm sorry. Is there anything I can do?"

"Ajit—please!" And Fran ran off down the hall.

That night Maggie ran into her sister's room, beaming with excitement. "So what happened? Did he ask you out? Why didn't you stop by the record store to let me know? I was dying of curiosity all afternoon."

"We had lunch together," Fran said flatly.

"So, aren't you thrilled? How did it go? . . . Hey, what's wrong with you?"

"He wants to *help* me, Maggie."

"What?"

"All he wanted to talk about was Aunt Jane and how much he wanted to help me break away from her influence."

"Well, so what? You need all the help you can get, right? Oh, I'm sorry, Fran, I didn't mean that. But is that all you're upset about? What's wrong with a guy who wants to help you with your problems? *I* could use a guy like that."

"Come on, Maggie, don't play dumb. You of all people should know that you can tell when a guy is really interested in you as a date and when he's not. Even *I* can tell that. And Paul just wasn't treating me like a date."

Just then the phone rang, and Maggie ran to answer it. Then she ran back upstairs and whispered, "Hurry, Fran, it's for you. I think it's him!"

Fran went to the telephone, trying not to let her imagination run wild.

"Hi, Fran, it's Paul Wingate. Look, did I say something wrong today? Because if I did, I'm really sorry. I really like you, Fran. I hope we can be friends."

"Sure, Paul. We can be friends."

"Just so you promise to give me another

chance. Look, I'll see you on Friday, okay? And I promise I won't even mention your aunt."

"Okay, Paul. Bye. See you Friday."

Maggie had been standing there the whole time, staring at her and trying to figure out what was going on. "Well," she said as soon as Fran hung up, "*what did he say?*"

"He wants to be my friend."

"Fran, he called you! That's a good sign! Did he ask you out?"

"He said he'd see me Friday at the bike shop. Please, Maggie, don't get my hopes up again. Paul's a great guy, but I just don't think he's attracted to me."

"Look, Fran, if you want my honest opinion, I think it's still too early to tell. But the *worst* thing you could do right now is keep feeling so down on yourself. I still say that underneath that bushy hair and baggy clothes, there's a terrific-looking girl waiting to get out. Why don't you give it a try?"

"Well . . ."

"I'll tell you what, Fran. We won't make a lot of changes right away. When I get out of work this afternoon, we'll just get you a couple of things. And I'll call Jenny, my hairdresser, right now so she can do something about your hair."

"My hair? What's she gonna do to it?" Fran sounded as if someone had just sentenced her to the guillotine.

"Fran, you have to get it out of your face. She won't do anything outrageous, but please let her do something. Don't worry. Jenny really knows how to cut hair. You won't be sorry."

Fran fingered a strand of her hair. "Oh, Maggie, I don't know."

"Trust me, Fran. You'll be thanking me for this when it's all over. Just trust me." Maggie picked up the phone and called Jenny the hairdresser for an appointment for Fran.

"You'd better be right about this," Fran mumbled under her breath, gazing nervously at the piece of hair she was twisting. "Please be right."

The next day after social studies, Fran was almost wishing for Ajit to show up so she could be detained. But miraculously Ajit wasn't waiting for her in the tangerine hallway, and Fran knew that there was going to be no way out of the 3:30 appointment Maggie had made for her with the hairdresser.

Fran had felt very self-conscious in the new outfit she had borrowed from Maggie—snug-fitting black jeans and a pink, short-sleeved blouse with delicate eyelet embroidery. She had even agreed to wear a pair of feminine sandals instead of her old running shoes.

At first she hadn't been sure how all this looked on her, and after she got off the bus in Harvard Square, she kept sneaking glances at herself in store windows and in the windows of parked cars. It wasn't that she didn't like what she saw, it was just that she wasn't used to seeing stylish clothes and a decent figure on herself. She was still afraid to admit to herself that maybe Maggie was right about her looks.

But then Ajit had made her feel even worse, gawking at her before class as if he'd never seen a girl before. He was so overwhelmed he could barely talk to her. Then, trying to be nonchalant, he had apologized for bothering her the day before and asked her if she felt better today. Fran tried her best to act normal and answer his questions, but he was making her nervous. He was really trying to act cool, but like her, he hadn't had much practice at it.

No one else seemed to notice any difference in her appearance, but that was little comfort to her. At three o'clock, she still felt uneasy about her "redecoration," and now she was really beginning to dread her appointment with Jenny.

Her head was full of images of blue and green hair, short, spiky hairdos, and fluffy Dolly Parton coifs. Slowly she dragged herself through Harvard Yard in the direction of Jenny's shop on Brattle Street, hoping that something like the sudden arrival of a hurricane would prevent her from making her appointment.

Fran's knees were shaking when she spotted Jenny's shop as she turned the corner onto Brattle Street. Then she had an idea. She'd walk by the shop first and look in. If she didn't like what she saw, she'd keep on walking and forget about the appointment. After all, she thought, she couldn't let someone with pink hair and a studded dog collar attack her.

But when Fran walked by the small salon, she was both pleased and disappointed. There was only one person in the place, Jenny, no doubt. She had long, straight blond hair, very lush but very natural looking. Fran couldn't see her face very well because Jenny was bent over a magazine and her hair fell over her profile. She was wearing a lime-colored French T-shirt and blue jeans.

Fran walked on by, then stopped short, pursing her lips and taking deep breaths. "Well, here goes nothing," she muttered.

She went back to the shop door and walked in, as rigid as a soldier. Jenny looked up from her magazine, a little startled. She had the bluest eyes Fran had ever seen. Then she smiled, and Fran could see how tiny and delicate her features really were, especially her button nose. She stood up and threw her hair over her shoulder. Everything about her was small and delicate, except for her fantastic hair. Instantly Fran saw her as a fairy princess, like Glenda the Good.

"Hi! You must be Fran, Maggie's sister." Her voice was high and sweet, and Fran immediately felt at ease with her.

"Yes," Fran said, giving her a shy smile. Maybe this wouldn't be too bad.

"Jenny, right?"

"That's me." She giggled. "Why don't you sit down here and we'll discuss this new hairstyle you want."

You mean the one my sister wants.

"Can I get you some coffee?" Jenny asked.

"Oh—no, thanks." Fran was too nervous about the impending haircut to hold anything down.

Jenny took a seat in the canvas chair next to Fran's. "I must confess, Fran. Your sister called me this morning with all kinds of instructions on what to do with your hair. But it's your head, and I won't do anything you won't be happy with."

This was exactly what Fran wanted to hear. She could feel the tension in her stomach disappearing already.

"Now," Jenny continued, "what do *you* want done with your hair?"

"Well, I don't know exactly. Maggie says it's always in my face, but I don't want a real short cut. I've always had it long. I'd feel naked if it was as short as Maggie's."

"I know what you mean. My hair has always been long, too. I think I'd go crazy if someone cut my hair in my sleep."

"Then you don't think it should be cut," Fran said hopefully.

"Well, I didn't say that." Jenny stood up and started to examine Fran's hair. "Your hair is awfully dry and fly-away, Fran. And these split ends are enough to make me cry. What I suggest is that I give you a conditioner and a henna rinse to bring out the highlights in your hair."

"Henna? I don't want to be a redhead!" Fran's stomach tightened up all of a sudden.

"There are all kinds of hennas, Fran. This one will just bring out your natural color."

"Oh."

Jenny reached in front of Fran and picked up her chin, examining her face in the mirror. She pulled the hair away from Fran's cheeks to get a look at the shape of her face. "You have a great face, Fran. You could do a lot of things with your hair."

"I could?" Fran was amazed to hear such a positive professional assessment of her looks.

"Well, you obviously don't have a very clear idea of what you want done with your hair, so why don't you leave it to me? I promise not to shorten it too much, and you can always stop me before I do anything."

Fran paused, comparing her straggly hair to Jenny's luxurious mane. "Well, you seem to appreciate long hair, so I think I can trust your judgment. As long as it won't be too radical, go ahead and do what you think is best."

"Okay. But don't look so worried. You'll be even more beautiful when I'm through.".

"Well, I don't know about beautiful—"

"Trust me," Jenny interrupted as she started combing out Fran's tangles. "You're gonna like this."

"I sure hope so." Fran sighed.

Chapter 9

"**W**ill you stop looking at me like that?!" Fran put down her coffee cup and made a face at her sister across the table.

Maggie just glowered at Fran in silence.

"Well, say something. What's wrong? You just keep staring at me like that."

Maggie just shook her head, her eyes never leaving Fran.

"Go on, say it! I look like a freak, right?" Fran was getting impatient with her sister's behavior.

Finally, Maggie spoke. "No, that's not it. The trouble is you look *too* good. I'm jealous. If I thought you were going to look *this* good, I would never have let Jenny loose on you."

"Oh, get out of here. You're just teasing me."

But it was true. Jenny had worked miracles with Fran's hair, shortening it to shoulder length and giving her bangs in place of her old part down the middle. She had managed to transform Fran's fly-away mop into a great casual style with shine and body. The cut was perfect for Fran. It framed her previously hidden face and showcased her big brown eyes. Fran had hardly believed it when Jenny had finished. She had never imagined she could look this good. But the big test would be on Friday—when she picked up the bike at Cambridge Cycles.

On Friday morning Fran borrowed a pair of Maggie's jeans and her red V-neck French T-shirt. But instead of Maggie's sandals, today Fran wore her own old blue-and-white running shoes.

"What are you wearing those for?" Maggie scowled down at Fran's feet. "You look terrific except for those."

"These are more comfortable for bike riding, and I'm wearing them," Fran said stubbornly.

"Okay, okay. I forgot about that."

"I don't even feel like me anymore," Fran said glumly. "I bet Paul won't even recognize me now."

"You're so dumb! You are you, the exact same person, only more so because now people can see what you really look like. Don't worry about Paul. He'll know who you are all right."

Maggie nodded suggestively, looking Fran over once again.

"And will you stop checking me out like that! You're worse than a guy."

Maggie giggled. "Sorry. I still can't get over it. Really, Fran, this is the best thing that could have happened to you."

Maggie's earnestness didn't relieve Fran's fears any. She still had a lot of doubts about the "new" Fran, and she couldn't resolve them in her mind. But the heavy footsteps on the back stairs interrupted her train of thought.

"H-e-e-e-r-e's Janie," Maggie muttered, imitating the nightly introduction for Johnny Carson.

Fran's heart was in her throat. Her aunt hadn't had much to say about Fran's hairstyle when she had first seen it on Tuesday night, and that bothered Fran. All week she'd been on the edge of her seat, waiting for some kind of criticism from her aunt. She was still waiting.

Jane burst into the kitchen, pumping her knees and pulling her sweaty T-shirt away from her skin to cool off.

"Good morning, ladies," she sang out. She seemed to be in a good mood; Fran and Maggie were immediately suspicious. Following her routine, she proceeded to the refrigerator for her oranges and began the morning health ritual. The only difference was that today she wore a big grin on her face.

Fran was convinced that something was up, but she wasn't sure what. Her aunt smiling was definitely a reason for concern. Fran shot her sister a quick glance. They knew this could be serious.

The electric juicer ground the helpless oranges mercilessly, but above the noise the girls could hear their aunt humming a tune. She hadn't been like this last night, Fran thought. Maybe she had fallen out of bed on her head.

When the last of the oranges had met its fate, Jane went on to her shoebox of vitamins to prepare her daily dosage. And she was still humming. Finally she sat down at the table with her morning fare. Maggie and Fran eyed her with stealthy glances.

"It's really a lovely morning," Jane chirped. "This is the kind of morning that makes jogging a real high."

"Really." Maggie was unimpressed and unconvinced that her aunt's current condition was runner's high.

"Oh, yes. This is the kind of morning that augurs well for a great day. A day for beauty and love."

Fran almost choked on her coffee. Love?! She wasn't sure she had ever heard her aunt use the word. Love was normally a frivolous word to her aunt, a word she would have traded in for a more sensible word.

"You're very—happy today," Fran finally ventured. "You—going somewhere today?"

"No, no place in particular. Maybe Harvard Square this afternoon."

"Oh?" Maggie prodded.

"Yes, I think I'll just treat myself today. Maybe go to the Peabody Museum. I haven't seen the glass flowers there in quite a while. Then I might browse around the book shops. Maybe. I don't know."

This was incredible. She was almost whimsical, and she was never whimsical.

"Maybe I'll stop by and see Janet at Emerson, Frances. Perhaps I'll see you there."

Maggie was beginning to look worried. Both girls wanted to feel Jane's forehead and check for fever.

"Well—ah, you know where I'll be, Aunt Jane." Fran didn't know what else to say. Searching for something to do, Fran glanced at her wristwatch. Quarter after eight. She thought of Paul at the bike shop and picking up Maggie's bike. All of a sudden her aunt's strange behavior took a backseat to her thoughts of Paul.

Will he like the new me? Will he notice? What will I say if he doesn't talk? What if he's not at work today? What if he just gives me the bike, and that's that—what do I do then? What if he starts talking about Aunt Jane again?

Fran began to fuzz out, a fretful expression

on her face. It was the direct opposite of Jane's delirium. Maggie frowned, feeling like an orderly in the loony bin.

"Oh, sister dear, didn't you say you wanted to go in early this morning? To study or *something?*"

"Huh?" Fran was still in a daze.

"I said, I thought you wanted to get to the square early this morning. Don't you have something you want to take care of before class?"

"Oh—yes. I guess I do." Fran gradually came out of her fog, wiped her mouth with her napkin, then stood up. "Yes, I have to look up something at the library," she announced for her aunt's benefit. "I'll see you two tonight, I guess. So long." Fran looked from Maggie to her aunt, expecting some kind of response.

"Yeah, take it easy, Fran." Maggie spoke quickly and impatiently, anxious for her to get on her way.

"Have a nice day, Frances," Aunt Jane sang out unexpectedly. "Maybe I'll stop by and see you this afternoon."

Her tone was oddly mischievous, and this disturbed Fran. There was no telling what the woman was capable of, Fran knew, but she couldn't worry about her now. Paul was on her mind.

"Bye," Fran murmured as she closed the door behind her.

On her way to the bus stop, Fran walked

like a zombie, lost in her thoughts about Paul and her doubts about this scheme to get his attention. When she eventually got on the bus, she couldn't stop looking at her faint reflection in the bus window, still uneasy about facing Paul.

This isn't me. Not really. Maybe this is all very dishonest. Tricking him with a pretty package when down deep it's the same old Fran.

Except maybe Maggie is right. This could be the real me, the one that used to hide behind being a brain.

Maybe this is all a lot of worry for nothing. I haven't changed, and I don't intend to. I'm just me, that's all. A haircut and some nice clothes don't change your personality or the way you think. Nothing can change that. Sorry, Paul. You'll just have to take me the way I am—if you want me at all.

Before she knew it, the bus had arrived in Harvard Square. It was a little after nine. The bike shop should have just opened for the day. It was time to go see Paul.

Fran jumped off the bus, full of determination and courage. But as she marched down the brick sidewalk, her boldness began to disappear, and she slowed her pace. Her take-it-or-leave-it attitude melted away as she realized how much she really liked Paul and why. He was sensitive, different. He was worth worrying about, she felt. As soon as she came up to Bow Street, she got the jitters, and butterflies were fluttering in her stomach. But she kept on going. Whatever happened, she wasn't sorry she had gotten to know Paul, and she wasn't sorry for trying to look as good as she could.

She walked up to Cambridge Cycles and paused for a moment, looking through the window. There was Paul, bent over Maggie's upside-down bike, tightening the spokes.

Maybe he wasn't finished with it, maybe she should come back later. . . . *Come on, Fran, don't chicken out now. Get going!*

Fran took a deep breath and pushed through the door of the bike shop. "Hi, Paul." Fran flashed him a tiny, nervous smile.

"Huh?" Paul hadn't noticed her come in, but when he lifted his head from his work, he practically did a double take. "Fran! Oh, hi!"

Fran could tell from the look on his face that he noticed the new hairstyle and clothes. It was obvious from his face that he liked it, which put Fran somewhat at ease.

"I came to pick up the bike, but I guess it's not ready yet. Maybe I should come back later. . . ." She reached for the doorknob.

"Oh, no, don't go!" Paul said quickly. "I'm almost finished. Just have to tighten a few more spokes. It won't take long."

"Okay." Fran smiled, pleased with his reaction to her, and started inching over toward him. She was delighted to see that he couldn't keep his eyes on his work and was constantly sneaking glances at her through the spokes of the wheel.

Fran wanted to say something, but she couldn't think of anything that wouldn't sound dumb. The quiet of the shop was beginning to make her nervous, and the click of Paul's wrench made her very aware of his presence even when she wasn't looking at him.

Paul finally broke the tension. "This is a nice little bike, Fran. I tried it out yesterday. Seems like a nice comfortable touring bike."

Fran wasn't sure how she should respond. "You mentioned that when I brought it in."

Paul stopped tightening for a second and looked up at her, a bashful smile on his face. "Yeah, I guess I did. Have you ever been touring?"

"No, I haven't."

"I go all the time. A couple of weeks ago, I rode up to Mount Washington in New Hampshire and back. Next summer I'd like to ride all over Europe."

"It sounds like fun. Where do you usually go when you tour around here?" Fran was genuinely curious.

"Everywhere. Down to the South Shore, all over Boston, Gloucester, Marblehead, Nahant, Charlestown, Wellesley. Sometimes I just start riding at random, looking for places I've never seen before. Makes me feel like an explorer."

"Wow, I'll bet it really is like being an explorer. I always wonder about the places you pass on the highway. They're just names to me, you know. But you really get to see what they're like. I think that's great."

"You do?" Paul sounded surprised. "Really?"

"Really!" she confirmed.

There was an odd moment of silence as if something magical was happening, but Fran couldn't figure out what it was. Then Paul spoke.

"Say, Fran—you wouldn't be interested in going for a—a ride around Boston with me—tomorrow?"

"What?" Fran couldn't believe what she had just heard.

"Just a short tour around Boston—nothing strenuous. If you want to, that is." Paul couldn't look at her now, his gaze kept falling to the floor.

"Do you promise we won't talk about my aunt?"

"Not if you don't want to. We've got plenty of time to find out more about each other."

Fran's eyes were sparkling with glee. She was giddy and dizzy—and in love. "I'd love to go with you, Paul," she whispered hoarsely.

"You would?" His face lit up like the sun. "Fantastic!"

"When?"

"Well, I get out of work at three tomorrow afternoon. Can you meet me here then?"

"Sure, no problem."

"From here we can cross the Anderson Bridge into Brighton, then—"

"Don't tell me, Paul. I want to be surprised." She grinned.

"Okay. Whatever you say."

"I can't wait."

"Do you want to leave your bike here until tomorrow?"

"Oh, that's a good idea."

"Great. That'll give me time to do some more adjustments for you."

Fran looked at Paul, wishing he would take her in his arms and kiss her. Paul might have been thinking the same thing from the way he was gazing at her. Fran started to blush.

"Well, ah, I guess I better get going, or I'll be late for class. So I'll see you here tomorrow at three?"

"I'l be waiting for you."

"Bye."

"Bye."

As soon as Fran had left the shop and passed the front window, she started to skip up Bow Street, delirious with the prospects of her first real date. She wished Music Towne were open so she could share the glorious news with Maggie. She was overflowing, giddy and ecstatic, like too much popcorn popping in a little pot.

Nothing can spoil today, she thought, floating off to class, *not the superbrains, not Ms. Goostray, not Ajit, not even crazy Aunt Jane. Because I have a date with Paul!*

Fran couldn't concentrate on anything but Paul all day, and she was glad of it. All she could do was daydream, planning the rest of her summer with Paul after her father returned from Ireland to liberate her from summer school. She stared out the window all morning at the bikes lined up in front of Cambridge Cycles, just thinking of Paul.

Lunchtime came, but she didn't want to go over and see him. She didn't want him to think she was too anxious. Not even wanting to risk running into him by mistake on Bow Street, she refrained from going to Music Towne to tell Maggie.

Even Ms. Goostray's dull class couldn't smother her excitement. But when she got out of social science, there was something waiting for her that she never expected.

Standing together in the tangerine hallway were her aunt and Ajit. Jane still had the same grin plastered across her face, and Ajit wore the tortured expression of unrequited love. Fran was suspicious the moment she spotted them. She considered ignoring them, but her aunt called out to her first.

"Frances! Frances! Over here!"

Fran regarded her aunt warily as she walked toward her and Ajit.

"Frances, I have a surprise for you." She beamed.

"What?" Fran's heart started to pound. This didn't look good.

"It took some doing, but I managed to get you two tickets to the Boston Symphony Orchestra performance tomorrow night. For you and Ajit. Isn't that wonderful?"

Fran's jaw dropped. She couldn't believe it.

"They're doing an all-Mozart program. You'll love it. Now it starts at seven-thirty, so I suggest you meet here in the square at six-thirty, at the Out of Town newsstand. That's the most convenient place for both of you. Is that all right with you, Ajit?"

"Yes, fine, Ms. Harrigan." He nodded vigorously.

"Good, then it's a date. Here are the tickets, Frances." Aunt Jane thrust the tiny envelope into Fran's numb fingers. "Now that's tomorrow evening at six-thirty in front of the newsstand. From there you'll take the Red Line train into Boston. You know how to get to Symphony Hall, Frances." Aunt Jane wouldn't let anyone else talk, she was so excited. "Well, I have to run now. I'll see you tonight, Frances. Goodbye, Ajit. I hope you enjoy the concert."

"I will, Ms. Harrigan, thank you."

Fran wanted to cry and kick and scream. The tickets were burning her fingers.

How could her aunt do this to her? It was incredible. Six-thirty! What about Paul? She couldn't cut her date short with him. She wouldn't. She didn't want to go to the stupid symphony with Ajit. She wanted to be with Paul.

But as usual, Fran kept her anger to herself, bottling it up in hopes that the situation would work itself out. She just stood there in the tangerine hallway, dumbfounded and sad, the tickets still stuck in her lifeless hand. Even if she did start yelling, now she wasn't sure who to scream at first—Aunt Jane for being so pushy, or lovesick Ajit for letting himself be used . . . or herself.

"So will I see you tomorrow at six-thirty, Fran?" Ajit asked timidly.

Fran didn't answer; she didn't know what to say. At last, biting her lip and looking down at the floor, she gave a slight, reluctant nod.

Chapter 10

"You mean she just set you up with him and *told* you that you had a date with him?" Maggie asked for the third time. "I can't believe it!"

"Yeah, she set me up all right," Fran moaned sadly. "I guess she thinks we're in love or something. No wonder she's been acting so mysterious ever since I got my hair cut. She really thinks she's doing me a favor."

"She really outdid herself this time. And I bet those symphony tickets set her back at least twenty bucks. What a waste." She just shook her head. "You and Paul could have gone to the Garden to see Blondie with that money."

"Who?" Fran growled, annoyed with her sister's casual attitude in the midst of the biggest crisis of her life.

"Never mind." Maggie smiled at Fran's ignorance. "So what are you going to do?"

"What can I do? I guess I have to cut my date with Paul short so I can meet Ajit in the square by six-thirty. Maybe Paul will let me leave the bike at Cambridge Cycles so I won't have to waste time coming back here."

"Boy, are you a dope." Maggie exhaled in exasperation. "That's a great way to turn him off. Don't you realize that? 'Can I leave my bike with you, Paul? I have to meet my other date now,' " she mimicked.

"Well, what do you suggest, Einstein?" Fran snapped.

"Give the tickets back to Aunt Jane and tell *her* to go with Ajit."

"I can't do that!"

"Why?"

"Because then I'd have to tell her why I couldn't go, because I have a date with Paul. And I know what she probably thinks of Paul. She's so crazy she's liable to call him up or go to the bike shop and tell him he's not good enough for me, just like she did with David Cooper." Fran's heart was pounding frantically.

Maggie stared right through her sister, lost in thought. She was trying to figure out how Fran could have her date with Paul and not let Jane find out. "Hmmmm. How creepy is this Ajit?" she finally asked.

"What?"

"Ajit. What is he like?"

"He's very intellectual, I told you."

"What else?"

"I don't know. Very polite and sort of formal, but kind of sweet really. If he wasn't a superbrain, he'd probably be a real nice guy."

Maggie exhaled deeply with resignation. "All right. Give me the tickets. I'll go with Ajit."

Fran's eyes widened, and her mouth fell open. "You? Go with Ajit? So I can be with Paul?" Tears brimmed in her eyes. She threw her arms around Maggie, not knowing how to thank her.

"All right, all right. Cut the tears before I change my mind. It's no big deal."

Fran looked at her sister intently. "Yes, it is. For me it is. And you know it. Thanks."

"Don't thank me yet. We still have to pull it off. And Aunt Jane still has a whole day to ruin things."

"That's true," Fran said distractedly. "But as tricky as she is, I don't think she is any match for you."

Maggie tried to hold back a grin, not wanting to let on that she was flattered. "Maybe so," she said cockily, "maybe so."

The next morning the girls were up early. Fran had no classes on Saturday, of course, but

Maggie had to be at work by nine. Fran wanted to see her before she left for work, just to run through the plan again. She didn't want any slipups that could ruin her date with Paul—like Maggie going to the wrong place to meet Ajit and Ajit calling her aunt to find out where Fran was. Maggie was too confident, Fran felt. That's why they had to discuss it again while Jane was out jogging.

As Maggie washed, dressed, and got herself ready for work, Fran hovered over her, grilling her on the plan, asking all her "what ifs," and expressing her doubts.

"Will you stop worrying?" Maggie threw her hands up as Fran followed her downstairs. "It'll work. Believe me."

"But what if she finds out?" Fran insisted.

"Then I'll make sure you have a nice funeral," Maggie quipped.

"This is no time for jokes!" Fran hissed. "You know how she—"

Maggie stopped short as she turned the corner and entered the kitchen. Fran looked up and gulped. It was Jane, sitting at the kitchen table, reading the morning *Globe* with a cup of black coffee steaming before her.

"Darn!" Maggie whispered.

"Morning, Aunt Jane," Fran announced nervously.

Jane emerged from behind the newspaper

and blinked like an owl. "Oh, good morning, Frances, Margaret." She went right back to what she was reading.

Maggie eyed her suspiciously, then looked at Fran, who just shrugged.

"You must have done your jogging pretty early this morning," Maggie commented casually as she poured herself a cup of coffee.

"Hmmm?"

"I said, you must have done your running earlier than usual today."

"Oh—no."

"You mean you've given up jogging?" Maggie persisted.

"No." Jane refused to lift her eyes from the paper.

"Injured?"

"No."

"Then why aren't you running today?"

"Because I'm running in a five-mile race this afternoon, if you must know, Margaret." She still wouldn't look up.

"Ah—where is this race?" Fran asked cautiously.

"Belmont," Jane snapped.

Good! Now I know where not to go bike riding.

"Well, I hope you win," Maggie said coolly.

"Margaret, I won't even finish the race if you keep disturbing me. I must compose myself before a race to calm my body. I'd prefer just to read the paper and relax, if you don't mind." Her eyes returned to the paper.

"Well, excuse me," Maggie muttered, wrinkling her nose again. She picked up her cup and nodded toward the hallway.

Fran took her cup and followed Maggie out to the front porch, where they could talk.

"Well, at least she'll be out of your hair today. She won't be able to bug you about what you're wearing or why you're leaving so early."

"Yeah. I knew her running mania had to be good for something."

"Now let's go through this once more. I meet Ajit at six-thirty in front of the Out of Town newsstand. The concert is at seven-thirty at Symphony Hall—"

"Right. You know how to get there?"

"Of course. Take the Red Line to Park Street, then switch to a Huntington Avenue train and get off at the Symphony Hall stop."

"Right. Now do you remember what I told you he looks like?"

"A superbrain."

"Be serious!"

"Indian. Dark hair, medium length. Dark eyes. Last name, Bannerji."

"Okay. And you're going to tell him that I wasn't feeling well so I sent you in my place."

"Got it." Maggie nodded in boredom, as if

she did this kind of thing every day. "Now how about you? You know what you're doing?"

"Don't be silly. Do you think I'd forget anything connected with my very first real date?"

"I suppose not. What are you wearing?"

"I don't know. Jeans, I guess."

"Wrong."

"What do you mean 'wrong'?"

Maggie sighed. "I knew you wouldn't think about clothes or anything like that." She shook her head.

"What's wrong with jeans and a top?" Fran asked innocently.

"It's just ordinary, that's all." She shook her head again. "Don't you want to look dynamite for this?"

"Well—I guess so. . . ."

"I figured you wouldn't have gotten yourself a new outfit, so I set aside something for you in my closet."

"What?" Fran looked skeptical.

"My maroon jump suit—the one with the short sleeves and short pants. It's comfortable but very sexy, perfect for a bike-riding date."

"Hmmm." Fran decided to reserve judgment until she tried it on.

"I left you a couple of barrettes on my bureau. Put one here and one here"—she indicated the right spots at Fran's temples—"so that your hair won't be all over the place when you stop riding and get down to business."

"Maggie!"

"Use some of my perfume, but don't use too much. Guys hate too much perfume."

"Anything else?" Fran said testily, feeling that Maggie was trying to redo her again.

"Just one thing."

"What now?"

Maggie leaned forward and whispered in Fran's ear. "Have a great time!" She gave Fran a squeeze and a smack on the cheek, then bounded down the porch stairs. "That's the most important thing of all," she called back.

"Okay. I'll see what I can do." Fran smiled back warmly at her sister.

"See you tonight." Maggie turned and trotted off to catch her bus to Harvard Square.

"Bye." Fran breathed a little easier, glad just to know that Maggie was rooting for her.

In all her nervous excitement, Fran had arrived too early in the square and had to kill time browsing in a book shop on Brattle Street until it was time to meet Paul. She had known that she was going to be early when she left Medford, but the silence in the empty house had made her uneasy. She was afraid that her aunt would hobble in at any moment, back early from her race because of a charley horse in her leg or something. Every time she heard a car door slam, Fran jumped, thinking that it

130

might be someone or something that could keep her from her date with Paul. It never crossed her mind that a car stopping at her house could be a cab bringing her father home. Somehow his return seemed like a long way off to her, although she had wished him home many times that week.

At ten to three, Fran started walking down Brattle Street, turning left on Mount Auburn Street and strolling down toward Bow Street. She was surprised at how calm she actually was, but as soon as she started to think about it, her calm dissipated and her stomach started to cramp. She stared up at the Bow Street sign, and a chill ran through her. But before she could even consider backing out, she glanced up the street at the bike shop. Paul was standing out front with his bike on his right and Maggie's on his left. He had spotted her first and was waving to her.

Trying her best to walk normally, Fran approached Paul. She was self-conscious about her walk, not knowing whether she should saunter over coolly or run up enthusiastically. Her walk didn't seem to bother Paul, though. He seemed happy just to see her.

"Hi, Fran." What a smile he had! Fran couldn't remember ever seeing him so openly happy, and she had spent a lot of time Paul-watching.

"Hi, Paul," she said, smiling, trying to hide her jitters.

"I like your jump suit. Perfect for touring. Looks nice on you." He couldn't keep his eyes off her.

"Thanks." Fran looked at the ground and blushed. It was the first time she had ever been complimented by a boy.

"I thought we might ride into Brighton, then head west out toward Wellesley—if that's okay with you."

"Fine with me," she said. *Just as long as I'm with you.*

"Okay. Shall we go?"

"Yup."

They mounted their bikes and rolled down the short incline of Bow Street, back onto Mount Auburn. Fran followed closely behind him, wondering whether her old three-speed could keep up with his fancy Italian ten-speed. She couldn't help but notice his long, muscular legs and his broad shoulders. She was a little embarrassed to be checking him out like this, but in his khaki shorts and navy-blue shirt, he was just too good to be true.

A date, she kept repeating in her mind, *my first real date.* The grin of delight just wouldn't leave her face.

As they came up to a busy intersection, Paul brought his bike to a halt and turned to

Fran. "Be careful here. The traffic is pretty hairy. Let's walk across Memorial Drive, then ride over the Anderson Bridge into Brighton. From there, we'll go down Harvard Street past Harvard Stadium."

"Okay." Fran nodded, listening carefully.

When the traffic light turned green, they pulled out onto Boylston Street and headed for the bridge. Paul was able to go very slowly with his well-balanced bike, slower than a casual stroll, something that was hard for Fran to do on her old bike. Nevertheless, Paul kept the pace even, constantly looking back to make sure she was all right in the wild Saturday traffic.

They crossed the bridge, and Paul watched her closely on the other side, where the traffic was even crazier. He hovered by her like a sheepdog, ready to act if anything unexpected occurred. Once they passed by the maniacal traffic of Soldiers' Field Road, an uncontrolled freeway that ran along the Charles River, and then the entrance to the Massachusetts Turnpike, they both breathed easier.

"Phew!" he commented as they pedaled down Harvard Street. "That's the only heavy traffic we'll have to deal with today—I hope." He smiled.

As the road widened and the harrowing traffic was left behind them, Fran began to feel very secure with Paul, impressed with his concern for her safety.

"Do you know where we are?" he asked.

"Sort of."

"Do you want the guided tour?"

"Oh, of course."

"Okay. Well, all this over here on the left is the Harvard Business School campus. And that on the right is Harvard Stadium."

Fran examined the old ivy-covered structure with the high classical arches all around its circumference. It looked like something she imagined might exist in England. "I never realized that part of Harvard was on this side of the river in Boston," she said.

"I guess I'm a pretty good tour guide then, huh?"

"So far, so good. What else are you going to show me?"

"You'll see." He laughed. "See that broadcasting tower way over there in the middle of that big parking lot?"

"Yeah."

"That's WGBH, the public TV station."

Fran stared off at the broadcasting tower and suddenly thought of all the "serious" television programs her aunt had suggested she watch that week. *This is no time to think about her!* Fran scolded herself.

They coasted on, weaving their way through a series of narrow residential streets until they came to a bridge that went over the Massachusetts Turnpike. They crossed it, then whizzed by several factories. They came to a hill, which Fran thought she'd never be able to pedal up until Paul pointed out that she should change gears. At the top of the hill, they came upon a square that Fran didn't recognize, where four busy roads intersected.

"Where are we?" Fran asked as they paused to wait for a break in the traffic.

"Union Square, Brighton."

"You really know where you're going, don't you?" Fran commented in amazement.

"Sure. It's no big deal, though. This is my hobby. I must have ridden through here a hundred times."

"I'm still impressed. I'm terrible with directions. I get lost in my own neighborhood."

"You? I don't believe it."

"It's true!" she insisted.

"Sure!" He laughed skeptically.

"I'm not kidding." She giggled. If anyone else had doubted her, she would have resented the implication that just because she was smart she had to know everything. But Paul was so casual and good-humored, she just knew he wasn't criticizing her.

When the traffic let up, Paul pushed off, and Fran followed him down a long residential street, past a small park, until they came to Commonwealth Avenue, which they followed straight up for about a mile to the Chestnut Hill Reservoir. Fran knew where she was now, and Paul seemed to read her mind when he turned into Boston College to cut through the upper campus where the beautiful old Gothic buildings were.

Paul didn't stop, but he kept a close watch on her as they crossed Commonwealth Avenue. She couldn't decide whether he was still very concerned for her safety or he just wanted to look at her. Either way she didn't mind one bit because whenever their eyes met, he flashed that warm smile of his.

After riding around Boston College, they headed for Newton. The houses here were newer and the neighborhood obviously wealthier than any they had passed so far. Occasionally Fran would slow down when an older, more unusual house caught her eye.

Soon they coasted into Newton Center with its multitude of tiny shops. Fran wondered where Paul would take them now, since there were several large streets to choose from here.

"Are you tired yet?" he called back to her.

"No way," she responded immediately. They had only been riding about an hour, and she certainly didn't want him to think she was frail.

"Shall we try for Wellesley?"

"Why not?" She grinned, willing to take on the challenge.

"You sure? It's not that close."

"I'm sure."

"Okay. Follow me."

He pedaled easily, and Fran pumped vigorously, eager to catch up to him. Finally she picked up enough speed to pass him, and she stuck her tongue out at him playfully as she whizzed by. Without a doubt, she knew she was having the best time of her life.

Chapter 11

By six o'clock, Fran and Paul were on their way back from Wellesley, winding through the back roads of Chestnut Hill. The houses here were even larger and more elaborate than the ones Fran had seen on Beacon Street between Newton and Wellesley. This had to be a very wealthy neighborhood, she figured as she gazed at walls of conservatory glass, greenhouses, and the carved marble columns in front of various houses. The area was dominated by towering oaks and elms that shaded everything. It was almost like another country, Fran thought, and suddenly she imagined herself touring the south of France with Paul.

Paul slowed down and looked over at Fran.

"Do you have to be back home at any particular time?"

"Midnight—I guess." Her father had set midnight as the weekend curfew for Fran and Maggie. Of course, Maggie was the only one who ever stayed out that late.

Paul nodded, squinting one eye like Popeye. "I guess I can get you back by midnight."

"Where are we going now?" Fran was excited now that she was sure there was more to come.

"Someplace special."

"Where?"

"You'll see."

Paul picked up his pace a bit and inched ahead of Fran. Soon they were back on a main road, Hammond Street. The traffic here forced Fran to drop back and trail Paul single file. They coasted down the slow grade of Hammond Street until they could see the Chestnut Hill Reservoir again in the distance. Now they came up to Cleveland Circle, where the trolley cars turned around.

Paul glanced back at Fran and grinned mischievously. Then without a word he guided his bike to the right, turning back onto Beacon Street and heading for downtown Boston.

Fran wasn't sure where he was going, but she was up for a surprise. All sorts of possibilities ran through her head as she tried to guess. Haymaker? The North End? Government Center? Beacon Hill? Chinatown?

Her curiosity was getting the better of her, and she was dying to know. "Paul," she called out, "tell me where we're going."

He just shook his head, grinning smugly.

"Oh, come on. Tell me!"

"Nope. You'll see soon enough."

They had gone about a mile or so down Beacon Street, past the Beaconsfield trolley stop, and were now approaching Coolidge Corner in Brookline. But then Paul suddenly stopped, waited for a break in the traffic, and crossed to the other side.

"Come on," he called back, making sure he didn't lose her. "We're almost there."

"Where?" Fran muttered, now totally confused because they were still pretty far from any of the destinations she had guessed.

"Just follow me."

He pedaled onto a side street. Fran grimaced as she surveyed the steep hill before her. What could be up there?

She started pedaling, but the hill was too much for her and her poor three-speed. "Hey! No fair," she called to Paul. "You've got seven more gears than I do. I can't make it up here."

Paul stopped and coasted back down to where she had given up. "Sure you can make it. Put your bike in third gear, then zigzag up the hill instead of trying to go straight up. Like this." He demonstrated the technique, swinging from one side of the empty road to the other.

Fran was skeptical, but when she tried it, she found that it worked. It wasn't easy, but it did work. She pumped and pumped, determined to make it to the top. When she reached the crest of the hill, she saw Paul standing over his bike, waiting for her at the edge of a small park overlooking the entire city.

"Welcome to Corey Hill Park," he announced. "This is my favorite spot in all Boston. You can see for miles from here."

Fran was very impressed. The view was nothing less than spectacular, especially because of the orange setting sun casting long shadows over Back Bay. The park was small, but it was perfect, she felt. Tall trees, benches, a swing set, seesaw, and this wonderful view. "Can we sit here for a while?" Fran asked enthusiastically.

"Of course. I wouldn't let you just walk away from here without really taking in this view."

They got off their bikes and wheeled them onto the grass. Paul picked out a big maple tree on a slope, and they set down their bikes and made themselves comfortable under its high, spreading boughs.

"This is incredible," Fran exclaimed, staring into the eastern vista. "How did you ever find this place?"

"I just stumbled on it by accident one Sunday a couple of weeks ago. I love it here."

"Me, too."

They started picking out all the landmarks they could. Then after a while she sneaked a glance at Paul's watch. It was almost six-thirty.

"Where's Harvard Square?" she asked out of the blue.

"It's—uh, over in that direction." Paul pointed back over Fran's shoulder. "But I don't think you can see it from here."

Fran turned around anyway and stared at the sky over Cambridge.

Maggie is meeting Ajit right about now. Is he going to be surprised! I hope it goes all right. He ought to be happy, though—Maggie's a real fox, as she would say. I just hope it doesn't get back to Aunt Jane.

Fran turned back to Paul and was startled to catch him staring at her. When he didn't avert his glance, she blushed.

"What are you thinking?" she asked.

"About you."

Fran looked at the ground, feeling her face grow hotter.

"Really," he continued, his voice soft and deep. "I was thinking about how different you are from all the other girls in our class. And about how dumb I was not to have noticed you before this summer. And about how I almost blew it at lunch the other day."

143

Oh, no, not again, Fran thought apprehensively.

"Fran, all I wanted to tell you that day was that I understood some of what you're going through. There's nothing wrong with being smart, Fran. I like you that way."

"You're just saying that," she muttered, her heart pounding in her chest.

"No—I mean it."

He reached out and gently lifted her chin. She searched his face, feelings of trust, love, fear, and longing glimmering in her eyes.

"Fran . . . can I kiss you?"

All of a sudden Fran couldn't think. Her lips just automatically went to Paul's, and her arms went around him. His kiss coursed through her like hot fudge running through her veins— slow and warm and sweet and good. She couldn't believe this was happening to her and that it just came so naturally, so easily. She felt she was watching herself in a movie, a movie about her falling in love with Paul.

But it was real, it was really happening. So perfect, so right, and she didn't even have to think about it.

Over an hour later, they were still sitting under that maple tree, Fran nuzzled into Paul's chest as he held her close, his cheek against her hair. They forgot about the time, staring at the magenta sky and the airplanes coming in and out of Logan Airport, blinking their green and red landing lights. Fran felt so good next to Paul she would have been happy to stay there forever. All her problems with Aunt Jane and summer school and the agony she put herself through about being doomed to the life of an intellectual just drained out of her. She felt free and completely at ease for once. It was as if she had just discovered fresh air.

"It's going to be dark pretty soon," Paul said softly, "and you don't have a headlight on your bike."

"No."

"I guess we'd better get going then. We should at least get past Harvard Square while it's still light." He sighed deeply. "I wish we didn't have to go, though."

Fran looked up at him. "Let's come back and camp out some night," she whispered.

"Camp out? In the middle of Brookline?" He laughed softly at the thought of it. "I'm sure the Brookline cops will love that."

Fran grinned sheepishly, nuzzling back into his chest. Paul bent his head, and they kissed once more. Fran was lightheaded all over again.

"I think we'd better go," he finally whispered.

"Oh . . ." she sighed. *Not now. Not yet!*

"We can come back—soon."

"Promise?"

"Promise."

"Okay."

As much as she didn't want to leave, Fran realized that Paul was right about riding while it was still light, so they brushed themselves off, mounted their bikes, and started back toward Medford. Paul led the way. There was not too much traffic until Harvard Avenue in Brighton, which was jammed with hordes of cars jostling for parking spaces around the numerous college hangouts in the area. They wove their way down the avenue, then found their way back to the Anderson Bridge and Harvard Square. The square was even crazier than Harvard Avenue was. Frantic drivers were zipping around corners to beat the next guy to a parking space. It was getting dark now, and the cars were switching on their headlights. Fran breathed a little easier when they were out of the square, heading toward Somerville and away from the awful Saturday night traffic.

Suddenly Paul slowed down and pulled over.

"What's the matter?" Fran asked, braking her bike. "We're almost home?"

"Are you hungry?" Paul asked eagerly.

"Well, yeah, but why are we—"

"You up for ice cream? *Steve's* ice cream?" Paul spoke as if he were referring to Ali Baba's treasure.

"Who's Steve?"

"You mean to tell me you've never had Steve's ice cream?!"

"No," Fran squeaked, feeling she should know about this place.

"Oh, we have to go, Fran. It's only the best homemade ice cream in the whole world. It's not far from here."

"It sounds great. But I thought you said we had to be back in Medford before dark."

"Well, yes, I did say that. But we aren't that far from home, and from here we can take roads with less traffic. I have a headlight. We can ride slow, and you can follow close behind. And I really want to take you to Steve's."

Fran didn't have to think about it at all. "Okay. Let's go."

Paul pushed off immediately, and Fran followed close behind. After a few blocks, Paul announced, "There it is. The place where the people are spilling out the door."

Fran couldn't believe what she saw—at least a hundred people were standing in line. And despite the long wait, this crowd was in pretty good spirits. It was almost like a big party, Fran thought, as they locked their bikes to a No Parking Anytime sign. She looked through the front window and saw a big, red, electric ice cream maker churning away, spitting bits of ice and salt as it worked.

"How did you find out about this place?" Fran asked as they took their places at the end of the line.

"Gee, I thought everybody knew about Steve's," Paul said matter-of-factly, then thought again, afraid that he might have offended her. "Well, everybody who's nuts for ice cream, that is."

Fran was touched to see that he was worried about her feelings. "This certainly looks like the right place for ice cream addicts," she commented. "This ice cream must be pretty special, huh?"

"It's out of this world. Everything here is homemade, including most of the toppings. And they'll put almost anything on your ice cream— m & m's, raisins, granola, crushed Heath bars, nuts, every kind of berry—oh, all kinds of stuff."

"I don't know what to have. It all sounds so good."

"Maybe we'll just have to keep coming back until you've tried all the combinations." He smiled and rolled his eyes, feigning innocence.

"Maybe," she said, laughing, "maybe."

The line started to move, and now Fran could see inside through the window. Steve's was shaped somewhat like a triangle with a barricaded walkway running along two sides. This was where the customers waited in line. All along the walkway, wire-mesh baskets full of bananas hung, adding to the bazaar atmosphere of the place. All along the knotty pine walls hung framed newspaper and magazine articles that raved about Steve's. And at the end of the walkway, just before the order counter, stood a vintage player piano. Fran could see the piano roll spinning over the reels, like a wringer on an old-fashioned washing machine. Every time someone opened the front door to enter or exit, Fran caught a few of its rinky-tink notes.

The line was moving quickly, and Fran and Paul were soon outside the door. The muted strains of the player piano could be heard through the door. The tune was familiar, but Fran couldn't remember the title.

"What's that song? Do you know?" She turned to Paul.

"I don't know. I've been wondering myself. It's very familiar." He bit his lower lip and looked at the ground, trying to concentrate.

Fran's gaze began to wander as she pondered the tune. Then she spotted a familiar person walking away from the cashier, holding a cone filled with a mound of ice cream covered with nuts and m & m's. It was Sam Patel, the math instructor from the summer school. Fran was astonished to see him in a place like this *and* with drops of melted ice cream clinging to his droopy mustache.

As soon as Sam came through the door, he spotted Fran.

149

"Hi, Fran." He grinned over his ice cream. "How ya doin'?"

"Fine," she said, a little nervous about seeing a teacher outside of class. "This is Paul Wingate. Paul, this is Sam Patel, my math teacher."

They exchanged handshakes and hellos, then Paul asked Sam, "Maybe you can help us out. We've been racking our brains, trying to remember the name of this song. Do you know it?"

"Hmmm." Sam knit his brows. "I really haven't been listening to it. Let me think."

Fran couldn't believe Paul had asked him that. She would never have asked a teacher something that frivolous. But to her amazement Sam didn't get angry or pass it off as triviality at all; he was thinking about it seriously!

"Gee, I don't know. But it's so familiar," Sam finally said.

"Yeah, that's what we were saying," Paul replied.

"This is going to bother me," Sam declared. "Hold on."

Sam turned around and went back in, weaving through the tightly packed tables and chairs to the piano. He found the piano roll's empty box on top of the piano, picked it up, and read the title. He was nodding with recognition and satisfaction when he came back out.

" 'Red River Valley.' "

"Of course!" Paul exclaimed.

"Oh, yes," Fran confirmed.

"Thanks," Paul said.

"Think nothing of it." Sam laughed. "If I didn't get that title, I know I would have been up all night trying to figure it out."

"Now if you'd just help me figure out what to order." Fran pointed to the blackboard over the cashier, where the long list of flavors and toppings were written in yellow, pink, and blue chalk.

"Oh, no, Fran. I can understand calculus, but all the possible combinations that you can derive from Steve's menu remain a delicious mystery to me. I can't help you with that one."

"Thanks a lot." Fran laughed, thinking what a wonderful, *regular* guy Sam was. She was beginning to realize there was nothing wrong with being smart as long as you didn't forget how to have fun.

"Well, I have to shove off," Sam said. "Nice meeting you, Paul. See you around, Fran." He gave them a wave and started walking down the street, his head bent over his ice cream.

"He's a nice guy," Paul commented after he left.

"Yeah. You'd never know he was a math teacher, would you?"

*   *   *

A half-hour later, Fran and Paul were seated at one of the ancient kitchen tables in the middle of Steve's, digging into their sundaes. Fran had ordered a single scoop of butter almond with granola, shredded coconut, and m & m's, and she had been surprised to see that at Steve's they mashed the toppings into the ice cream instead of just sprinkling them on top. After just one bite, she knew she was in ice cream heaven.

Paul had two scoops—one coffee, the other carob—with hot fudge, cashews, and crushed Heath bar. Paul dug into his sundae, but his attention was focused on Fran. He couldn't stop looking at her.

"Want to try some of mine?" he offered.

She looked up and giggled, licking a piece of coconut from the corner of her mouth. "Sure. Try mine, too."

They lingered over their sundaes, staring into each other's eyes until the ice cream was gone. Paul got up eventually and fetched two paper cups of water for them. Then he looked at his watch.

"It's getting late," he said, a melancholy note in his voice. "I guess we'd better get going."

"I suppose so." She sighed, disappointed that their date had to come to an end.

They stood up reluctantly, neither one in any hurry to leave. But as Fran threw her empty ice cream cup and plastic spoon into the trash can, she grinned to herself, imagining how sweet their good night kiss would be.

Like having sundaes all over again . . . but better.

Chapter 12

It was almost eleven o'clock when Fran and Paul got back to her house. When he hoisted her bike up on his shoulder and brought it up the front stairs for her, she felt a bit sad because their date was ending.

"Do you want to lock it?" he asked, setting it against the banister.

"I'll do it later," she replied quietly, standing behind him in the shadows.

Paul turned to her and took both her hands in his. "Well . . . I guess I better be going. . . ." He didn't sound as if he really wanted to leave.

"I had a wonderful time, Paul. Thanks." Fran's eyes glistened in the dark.

Paul's face was hovering close to hers, and

Fran knew they were both thinking the same thing. "I did, too. . . . I—ah—"

Just as Paul was about to put his arms around her, the porch lights flashed on, and they heard the front door opening. It was Jane Harrigan, standing behind the screen door.

"Frances!"

Fran's body stiffened. She was torn between rage and embarrassment. There was no time to think, though, and the tears welled instantly in her eyes.

"Frances, where is Ajit? You were supposed to be with him tonight."

Fran's face turned crimson, and her stomach was rolling. *She's doing it again. Just like with David Cooper. She's doing it again!*

She tried valiantly to remain composed and deal with her aunt without crying. "Aunt Jane, this is Paul—"

"I know who *he* is," she cut Fran off abruptly. "What I want to know is where Ajit is! You had a date with him tonight. I thought—"

Fran's throat constricted. She couldn't talk. A big tear rolled down her cheek, and Fran bent her head to hide the coming flood.

"Ms. Harrigan, I—"

"I'm not talking to you, Mr. Wingate!"

Fran just wanted to die. She couldn't believe that the most wonderful day of her entire life was going to end like this. But before her aunt could say anything else, the sound of approaching footsteps on the front walk caught her attention. It was Maggie and Ajit, walking hand in hand.

"Oh, boy . . ." Maggie mumbled under her breath as soon as she saw the gathering on the porch.

"Good evening, Ms. Harrigan." Ajit smiled, unaware of what was happening. "Hello, Fran. I hope you're feeling better."

"What was that, Ajit?" Jane asked, softening her harsh tone for Ajit, who looked very confused now.

"Well—Fran was ill. That's why Maggie took her place tonight, of course."

Maggie blew her cheeks out and shut her eyes.

Jane's nostrils flared. "You deceived me! Both of you!" she declared in a loud but steady voice. "I did not buy those symphony tickets for your sister, Frances. They were for you and Ajit. I thought the two of you would have a beautiful evening. I'm absolutely ashamed of you girls. I can't tell you how upset I am with you."

"But there's no reason to be upset, Ms. Harrigan. Maggie and I had a great time together. We returned the tickets at the box office and went to the baseball game instead. I'm very glad Maggie suggested it. You know, I'd never been to a Red Sox game before. I loved it."

He smiled at Maggie, still holding her hand.

Fran was quite surprised to see this, wondering just how well they really did get along. But more than that, she was impressed with Ajit for standing up to her aunt again.

He wasn't such a nerd after all, she thought, then glanced over at Paul, who was looking at her with a pained, sympathetic expression. What must he think?

Jane sighed and folded her arms. "Ajit, I'm very sorry this happened. I apologize for both my nieces, and I promise to make this up to you."

"There's no reason to be apologetic, Ms.—"

"Please, Ajit. I think you should go now."

Ajit just sighed and looked longingly at Maggie. "May I call you soon, Maggie?"

Maggie nodded and managed a slight smile.

He grinned hopefully at that. "Good night, Maggie. I had fun." Then he pecked her on the cheek, lingering for a moment. "Good night, everyone," he said, heading down the front steps. On the bottom step he paused and looked up at Maggie forlornly, his liquid brown eyes full of anxiety.

"Go ahead, Ajit," Maggie said. "I'll be okay."

As Ajit reluctantly walked off, Jane turned to Paul. "As for you, Mr. Wingate, your parents will be hearing from me about your shameful behavior."

"What shameful behavior?" Paul spoke calmly, but it was obvious that there was anger building up inside him.

"Don't be coy with me, young man. You know exactly what I'm referring to."

"No, I don't, and neither do you."

Jane looked as if she'd been slapped. She was definitely losing her cool over this. Fran felt sorry for her, but she was proud of Paul for speaking up.

"I'm asking you politely to go home, young man," Jane said desperately. "I want to talk to my nieces alone."

Paul ignored her and turned to Fran. He took her hand and lifted her tear-stained face. "I won't go unless you want me to," he whispered.

She wiped her puffy eyes with the back of her hand. "Go on home, Paul," she said, sniffling. "Please. I'll talk to you in the morning."

"Are you sure?"

"Yes."

Paul hesitated for only a second before he leaned forward and kissed her lightly on the lips. "I'll call you," he said softly. "It'll be all right," he said to Fran, then turned down the steps and went for his bike lying on the lawn. He mounted his ten-speed, but before he left, he looked up at Fran once more. "Good night, Fran. So long, Maggie." Then he pushed off and slowly pedaled away.

"Into the parlor," Jane ordered as soon as

Paul's headlight was out of sight. "You have a lot of explaining to do."

Maggie shook her head and smiled. "Don't let her shake you," she whispered to Fran. "As long as you had a good time with Paul, that's the only thing that matters."

"I'll never forgive you two for this prank," Jane said. "Of course, this is your style, Margaret. I've come to expect this sort of thing from you. But I'm surprised at you, Frances. You're more intelligent than this. You should have known better."

Fran was too tired to get angry. She was sorry her aunt had had to find out about Paul this way. But it was her own fault. She had pushed Fran and Maggie into tricking her. But before she could say anything, they were distracted by the sound of a car pulling up in front of the house. It was a taxi. They all went to the window to see Jack Pastore emerge from the cab, his trench coat over one arm, his flight bag in the other.

"Thank goodness," Maggie muttered. "Just in time."

"Excellent," Jane said. "Your father should be part of this."

But neither Fran nor Maggie heard this, for they were already out on the front porch, greeting their father.

"Thank God you're here, Dad," Maggie said, throwing her arms around him. "How was your

160

trip? I'm really glad you're back. We were just about to run away from home."

"What?!" Jack Pastore's tired eyes suddenly were alert, and a look of concern came over his face. Then he noticed Fran's puffy red eyes. "What's going on?"

Twenty minutes later Mr. Pastore had heard Jane's detailed story on the girls' awful behavior and her suggestions for appropriate punishment, as well as Maggie's heated accusations concerning Jane's bullying of Fran.

Mr. Pastore had leaned against the radiator throughout, his arms crossed over his chest as he weighed their arguments. It broke his heart to have to hear all this. There was no reason for this kind of anger in a family, he felt. He rubbed his chin, trying to make sense of it all, now that he had been forced into the thankless job of arbitrator. It seemed inevitable that someone would walk away from this with a lot of hard feelings, and he would be blamed for his decisions. He sighed deeply, looking from his younger daughter to his sister-in-law.

"You say the girls have been disobedient and deceptive, Jane. Maggie claims that you've been insensitive and authoritarian." He sighed and looked to Fran. "What's your side of the story, Fran?"

Fran had been sitting on the couch, listening to her sister and aunt shout at each other.

The whole scene had made her very uncomfortable. She had wished she could just disappear. Now, as she looked up at her father, she noticed that his brow was furrowed and that there was sadness in his face. He seemed to be begging her for some kind of rational explanation. She suddenly felt they were all forcing him to make a choice, to take sides with either her and Maggie or Aunt Jane. She knew it wasn't fair to him. And a pitched battle wouldn't solve the problem.

"Dad, the problem isn't who's right or wrong," Fran started quietly. "It's a matter of misunderstanding."

"Come on, Fran. Take a stand," Maggie protested. "Tell him what a witch she's been."

"Frances knows very well that I'm only concerned with what's best for her," Jane snarled from her armchair.

"Can I talk for myself, please?" Fran stared them both down. "See, Dad, this is the whole problem. Certain people seem to think that I'm helpless, that I have to be pushed into things. Everybody means well, but I just end up getting more confused. Aunt Jane thinks I'm just a brain. She doesn't realize I'm a regular teenager, too, who needs to have fun and make my own decisions. So she made me go to this advanced summer school, even when I didn't want to go. And I was too scared to say anything until Maggie set me straight about a few things. As a matter of fact, if it wasn't for Maggie, I'd just be

162

going along with everything Aunt Jane wants for me, and I'd be miserable. See, I just want to be normal, Dad. I don't mind being smart, as long as I can still go to Medford High in September and be Paul Wingate's girlfriend. Is that too much to ask?"

"I'm disappointed with you, Frances. What kind of goals are those? It will be a crime to waste potential like yours!"

Fran stared pathetically at her aunt. "I realize you only want good things for me, Aunt Jane, but you go overboard. You want me to be something I'm not."

"But you have a high IQ. You have excellent grades. You can—"

"But I'm not happy!" Fran insisted loudly. Her aunt was silenced by her heartfelt plea. "Don't you understand that? Your master plan for me is ruining my life. I have to make my own choices. Why won't you let me?"

Jane's lips began to tremble. Quickly she removed her glasses and wiped the emerging tears from her eyes. "When your mother died," she said, beginning to sob, "I vowed that I would do everything I could for you two. I know I'm not the motherly type, but with you, Frances, I felt I had someone I could do a lot for. I wanted you to have the best educational opportunities possible. I wanted you to have the best—really. It's not that I love Margaret any less. It's just that I felt I could do *more* for you, that I could make you excel. Your mother would have wanted that!"

Fran looked at her imploringly. "Would she have wanted me to be unhappy?"

Aunt Jane had no answer for that. She buried her face in her hands and wept silently.

Fran stood up and went to her, embracing her.

"I only did what I felt was best. I didn't want to hurt you," Aunt Jane whispered pleadingly. "I never thought I was pushing you into anything. Will you forgive me?"

"You don't even have to ask, Aunt Jane." Fran hugged her tight and kissed her on the cheek.

"Boy, this is heavy," Maggie murmured, wiping a tear from her eye.

Mr. Pastore spoke softly. "Well, it looks like Fran has solved the problem for us. Fran, I want to thank you for preventing a family war. You're much wiser than your years."

"But, Dad," Fran objected, her arm still around her aunt, "we *haven't* solved everything. What about summer school? And the job at the *Globe*?"

"It seems to me that you've already made up your mind about quitting summer school. As for the apprenticeship at the *Globe*, you don't have to worry about that until the personnel department decides to take you."

Fran looked to her aunt.

"You know what you want," her aunt said, smiling, "and I promise to respect your decision. Anyway, I have a feeling you'll get the job at the newspaper, and that will be excellent experience for you. Experience can be just as important as what you get in the classroom."

All of a sudden Fran felt as if a heavy boulder had been lifted from her shoulders. She was at ease, self-assured. Everything seemed to be falling into place now. Except for one thing.

"What time is it, Dad?" she asked suddenly.

He looked at his watch. "It's quarter to twelve," he replied.

"I wonder if it's too late," she said.

"Yes, but this is an unusual circumstance." Maggie smiled knowingly.

Fran nodded slowly, then stood up and went to the kitchen. Immediately she picked up the receiver of the wall phone, then replaced it while she looked up the number in the phone book.

It rang three times before anyone answered.

"Hello, Paul? Did I wake anyone up?"

"No. My parents are out. Are you okay, Fran?"

"Yeah. Luckily my father came home, and we straightened things out. I want to apologize for what happened—"

"You don't have to apologize. We had a great time today. I'd just as soon forget about your aunt and remember the rest of the day."

"I had a wonderful time, too. I didn't really get to thank you, though."

"Oh—well, you know . . ."

"Paul, are you busy tomorrow?"

"No."

"You wouldn't like to go riding again tomorrow, would you?"

"Sure I would!"

"You would?"

"Yeah! You know, I was thinking. Mr. Prince has a bicycle built for two at the shop. I'm sure he'd let us borrow it for the day. I've got a key to the shop, so getting it won't be a problem. What do you think?"

"Fantastic. I can't wait."

"Shall I pick you up, say, around one?"

"Perfect."

"Maybe we could go back to Corey Hill Park—if you'd like."

"I was hoping you'd suggest that." Fran blushed.

Paul chuckled nervously. "Then I'll see you tomorrow. Okay?"

"Right. Bye now."

"Good night, Fran."

She hung up the phone, a dreamy grin on her face. *I guess I'm just a normal teenager after all*, she thought.

Read these great new
Sweet Dreams romances

of lies and confusion—until the night when her lies go too far.

#17 ASK ANNIE by Suzanne Rand
(#22518-9 • $1.95)

At first, Annie was thrilled to give Tim advice about his girlfriend—until he asks Annie how to keep beautiful, stuck-up Marcy in line. If she helps Tim keep Marcy, Annie will never get a chance with him. But if she doesn't, will Tim stop being her friend?

#18 TEN-BOY SUMMER by Janet Quin-Harkin
(#22519-7 • $1.95)

Jill's vacation gets off to a wild start when her best friend, Toni, thinks up a contest—who can be the first to date ten new boys! It seems like a great idea until Jill meets Craig and knows she's in love. If Jill drops out of the contest, she won't be able to face her best friend. If she doesn't, she'll lose Craig forever.

And make sure to look for these
Sweet Dreams romances, coming soon: